MADISON

VENGEANCE IS MINE

A. V. SMITH

Book Cover: Seviinth Degree Production, LLC

Consulting Editor: Kristin Reeg

Editor: Tricia Barnes

Warped Writing and Publishing LLC, Columbus, Ohio

ISBN: 978-1-7351069-7-7

DEDICATION

To my children, Devan, Naiya and Christian:

My prayer to The Universe for you has been sent. You are my life source; greatness awaits you.

I Love You.

ACKNOWLEDGEMENTS

"To God The Universe I hear the words you send. I submit."

To the Jefferson, White, and Burton ancestors: Because of you, I am.

My parents, Diane and Irvin: a child grows best in a stable foundation. Thank you for pushing us to be better every day. I love you.

Fred Jefferson"Pops": Your support and love spreads through me and your grandchildren.

To the memory of departed father Roger Smith, life lessons are learned sometimes in the strangest circumstance.

Auntie Charlotte Burton: Our elder, I have always known our history and love through your voice.

My siblings: Portia White; Rod Smith; Irvin White III; Troy Smith; (Donald, Cameron and Marcette): I can't imagine a day of my life without knowing the greatness of you.

The Alvarez Family, Ramon and Leticia; thank you for sharing an abundance of peace and love along with the history of the family. Gisela Alvarez, thank you our connection of life experience and support during the entire process.

Mary Hoffett; Richard Higgins; Cynthia Stocksdale; Brandon McNeal; Erin and Tony Myers; Valerie Jenkins and Pam Wentz.: Thank you for shining a light in my dark hours.

Vernell Bristow, Carlitha Martez-Allen, Graciela Patino and Elaine Shady Carter; Teena Berberick for support each step of the way.

82879

∞

TABLE OF CONTENTS

EXHALE. DOUBLE TAP. BODY DROPPED.

The large warehouse was occupied with those who could be trusted. Scores of men and women congregating together, waiting to receive their orders. The bright lights inside gave no comfort of how dark the night would become.

The tables scattered throughout the lower level of the space were completely covered in guns and ammunition. The Ak-47 seemed to be the weapon of choice for many. M-16 assault rifles not yet claimed were being checked, and cartridges filled.

The air was thick, as was the cigarette smoke, and the tension could be cut with a knife. "It's Funky Enough" by the D.O.C was playing loudly in one corner of the warehouse and it carried the music throughout.

"Let me hit that." A cappuccino skin woman with shoulder length cornrows approached a group of four older teens gathered around the base of the stairs, leading to the second level where decisions were being made.

She took the Philly blunt and inhaled deeply, trying not to cough, but it was futile.

"That's that shit Yvonne, you used to smokin that dirt." One of the teens laughed. His hair, low and tapered, was freshly cut with waves being formed. A shade darker than she was, his teeth were sparkling white.

"Maybe, but I'm smokin this right now ain't I Caine, or you got something to say Vance?" she paused, pursing her lips before staring at another male in the group.

"Nothing?" She waited and then inhaled another large portion of the marijuana, patting her chest attempting not to cough again.

"What are you looking at Monster?" she redirected her next few words to the final member of their party. The tallest of the teen boys who had remained quiet, only looking up after re-checking his tactical vest. He simply shook his head and ignored her.

"Give me that shit. You need to keep yo head straight. Look around; Unc ain't upstairs deciding where the family picnic is gon be. B. Fred why is your sister here anyway?" Caine asked.

"I'm right here, don't be talking like I ain't standing right here…" Her voice trailed off as everyone's attention was drawn to the second level where two men and a woman walked out of the office first, followed by a tall and burly man, Uncle Harold; the head of this 'family'.

The shot callers had come to an agreement. It was war.

No additional words needed to be spoken. Those weapons that had remained on the tables had been taken and vans were loaded up. The capitol city of Ohio would forever be changed during this last year of the 80's.

Bob sat with his cousin Vance, and his two best friends since second grade, in the back of the old Ford Conversion Van. He never trusted anyone outside of these three and their last companion, Lonnie. Caught up in the crossfire of a rival gang infringing on their territory earlier, Lonnie was recovering after being shot and left for dead.

Now a show of force was the only adequate response.

Bob looked at Caine and Monty, all four were leaving for the military in two days. They understood the risks involved, but when his Uncle called for bodies, everyone mobilized.

"These muthafuckas gon die, ya heard?" Bob checked his AK-47, both handguns in his possession and made sure he chambered a round. He handed a second pistol to Caine.

"Everybody dies." Caine nodded and tucked the .9mm into his waist before laying his M4 across his lap.
Barely eighteen, this wasn't the first episode of retribution he participated in, but now, since learning he

and his girlfriend were going to be having a baby, he was focused on providing a better life for his unborn child than he had.

"Yo B, don't be yelling out that B Fred. said what's up." Monty laughed loudly, causing the rest congregated in the space to laugh, even though the tension was high.

"Nah fool, that's some dopeness, you just hatin as usual." Bob then pointed to Monty's gun to check the safety was off.

"Check all yo shit Monster, Sheila ain't turning into Barbara Jean on my ass." Bob then made eye contact with each of them, they were brothers and they were trained for this.

"Y'all be ready to pop these fools, run up in that bitch and don't none of em see tomorrow. They all gotta die!" The voice carried into the back of the van from the driver, as he looked into the rear-view mirror to make eye contact with each person present.

He kept one hand on the steering wheel and one on the

gun in his lap, finger resting in a ready position.

There were another seven vans like this moving deliberately in the hours after midnight. Each one set to hit a different stash house of Paris Crisp, who sat at the head of the rival gang. Paris had set his eyes on the entire state and Bob's uncle and his East side gang were the last group standing in the way of his first conquest, Columbus, Ohio.

Other vehicles were scarcely seen on the road as midnight came and went and the teens pulled closer to their target Silence had been the foregone conclusion and now only focus showed in their eyes. This group had been assembled and trained by Uncle Harold and his lieutenants for the past five years. They were treated like men at an early age in this regard. Vance being Uncle Harold's son, and Bob his nephew; though not related, Caine and Monty were equally considered family.

"Buck up." The driver put a bullet in his chamber and rolled his window down. He turned the lights to the van off as they made their final approach.

"We all make it back, let's go!" Caine pulled his ski-mask down leaving only his eyes visible. Following his lead, the rest repeated the action.

He put his hand on the interior door as they slowly advanced towards the house.

The driver spotted two guys sitting outside the stash house in a Chevy Impala as someone sparked a lighter.

He flashed his high-beam lights to blind them.

"You sum hoe ass ..." he fired his .45 caliber pistol into the car before they could respond.

Caine was first to emerge from the van. He took aim at someone running from the rear of the house. His M4 was a gift from Uncle Harold for saving Yvonne from being kidnapped a few years prior.

"Exhale. Double tap. Body dropped." Caine advanced as chaos erupted.

Flashes of light contrasted against the darkness of the night. Glass from the up-stairs windows of the stash house were broken from the inside, as bullets rained down in their direction from weapons similar to theirs.

"Advance." Caine called out, and the four men moved forward to get out of the line of sight of those shooting downward. Two more men exited the front door. Bob had taken cover behind the Chevy Impala and shot both men, who fell down the porch stairs.

"Move!" Monty touched Bob on the shoulder to indicate he was moving and to cover him before following.

Vance moved in tandem from the opposite side of their position. He took a frag from his vest, pulled the pin and tossed it into one of the upstairs windows. When it exploded the team of four broke through the front door and were met with resistance.

Caine shot the first person he saw, a man rounding the corner with a shotgun in his hand. Vance entered and flanked left as Caine moved forward. The other two entered and killed everyone.

They took the drugs and money on site and left as the

sounds of sirens were heard in the distance.

When they arrived at the rendezvous, only four of the other vans had returned.

"Dad, a tribute." Vance dropped the bags of money and drugs onto the table where his father sat.

His father nodded at the group of four with a large bottle of Hennessy in his hand. He took a swig and winced. His eyes looked tired.

"Jazz and his squad didn't make it. P. Crisp was on site and there were extra guards. They took out a general and two lieutenants. P. Crisp got shot too, I'm waiting on details to finish him off tonight."

Uncle Harold waved the group of four forward.

He handed Vance the bottle, who took a swig and passed it to his friends.

"I never wanted this for any of you, your work is done until you get back from serving your country." Uncle Harold stood and walked to the group of four.

"The only way to win in this game is to trust no one, but if I had this, this connection like the four of you, I'd disagree."

Commotion was heard from outside the room they occupied.

Another member entered the room with a bit of excitement in his voice.

"Unc, P.Crisp is dead and they're all scrambling."

Uncle Harold took a deep breath. He had already lost upper members of his organization, but his ambition knew that lives had to be lost in the conquest to bring his family more power.

"Unc, if I can say something." Caine interjected slowly.

"I never intend to speak out the pocket but right now if we hit the rest of them, you'll have the city under your control before the sun rises tomorrow morning."

Bob and Vance agreed while Monty took another sip

from the liquor bottle.

"Yeah he's right." Vance chimed in.

"Unc, let us give you the city before we leave." Bob agreed and took the bottle from Monty. He took a huge gulp and passed it along to the two others.

"I have given you my blessing to not participate in this shit, but you four always have the best interest of the family." Uncle Harold snatched the bottle from Vance and raised it.

"Family Always."

Everyone present repeated their mantra.

"Go bring me the muthafuckin city!"

For the next several hours the capital city of Ohio turned into a battle ground resembling overseas conflict waged by Sovereign nations.

Police sirens filled the night along as more dead bodies

were found. Both city helicopters occupied the night sky.

The war had already been won, but those remaining from P. Crisp's gang didn't realize it until the early morning hours.

When it was all said and done, the last two generals and several lieutenants from the rival organization had been murdered; the word was already passing through the criminal underbelly that power had changed hands, and Uncle Harold let it be known any thought of retaliation would be met with the full force of his hand.

Vance and his group of four had been silent with no one hearing from them, only that they had completed their task as seen on the breaking news. Their target stash house was burned to a crisp with fire trucks on site attempting to put out the blaze.

Uncle Harold sent out a few women to scout the city for word about his son, nephew and the two others he let lead men into harms way. The four boys had always wanted to prove their 'metal' being surrounded by bangers who were in and out of prison. When you were family, there was no higher honor for Uncle Harold, and he treated you as such. He had protection for those who had to do bids inside local jails and state prisons. Family and loyalty; both equal when weighed on the scale.

An older model year Ford Expedition was let in after Bob was identified as the driver.

The driver side door opened, and Bob got out and opened the rear driver side door as Monty stepped out. Caine exited the rear passenger side door and walked to the other side with Bob and Monty who stared into the backseat.

All three older teenagers were covered in blood.

"Unc! Unc! Uncle Harold!" Caine called out and then ordered Bob and Monty to help him.

Caine reached into the Expedition and slowly started pulling the lifeless body of their brother out.

"No! No! No!" Uncle Harold stood from the second level staring down as they placed Vance's body on one of the tables situated in the open space.

The Patriarch moved swiftly down the stairs while keeping his eyes on his son's dead body.

The silence in the space was deafening.

Everyone understood that lives would be lost during the city takeover, but none expected this result.

Everyone else stood back away from the table, except the three older teens as Uncle Harold approached. His face showed anguish and bewilderment.

"Unc, we are sorry and take responsibility." Caine spoke up. Excuses were tools of incompetence and Uncle Harold did not push this group of four to be ordinary.

Uncle Harold walked around the table on which his son's dead body lay. He touched his hand and then opened his shirt where he had been shot in the chest by a shotgun. His tactical vest had not stopped the bullet.

The teens didn't say anything. They were uncertain what their fate would be.

"What happened?" His voice shook with his overwhelming emotion.

Bob gave the first-hand account.

"We smoked the last stash house and was making our way back to the van when two cars pulled up with P Crisp crew wanting retaliation. They banged Billy Buttons in the van, and we had to take cover back inside the house. Vance entered first and was shot from a small group coming in the back of the house with heavier weapons. He took one blast to the chest before returning fire. The vest didn't save, the slugs were heavy...we couldn't save..." Caine's voice got lost in response.

"We secured the house and tried to save him Unc, we tried to save him." Bob stood squarely in front of his uncle, as did Monty and Caine. The three teenagers had tears streaming down their faces, but they stood upright, like men without making a sound.

In Vance, they had lost more than a friend, they had lost the best of them.

"He would've chosen to die with you by his side, each of you. I've gained the city at the expense of my son…" He took a few steps to close the distance between himself and the three in front of him.

He walked to each and looked at them with tears also in his eyes. His voice pushed the words out.

"My heart breaks for the son I have lost on this day. He was the best of each of you rolled up in one and the worst of himself, I hold myself accountable."

Uncle Harold pulled all three boys into his arms and embraced them before pulling back.

"These three have earned the right to counsel now and forever!" These eleven words he uttered would change their lives forever.

Now that Uncle Harold controlled the capital city, law enforcement and politicians would be his new comrades. He would need counsel and none as young as these three had ever been awarded a prestigious rank like this. They would be away serving while everything got sorted out.

"We have time to honor my son. Right now, his sacrifice will not be in vain. I had Yvonne and Raindrop summon those subsidiaries of P. Crisp. I'm fair and will give them their new terms. I need you all with me. When this is done go home to your people and get ready to leave all this behind."

Three Chevy Suburbans were loaded up with his most skilled guards. The remote location where P. Crisp merchandised was at a building being developed as an attachment to a local grocery store.

When they walked into one of the conference rooms, four people set at the table. Three men and one woman; behind each of them stood a guard with a pistol in hand.

"So you were behind all of this? I never thought you had ambition on such a grand scheme." The woman sat in a Cincinnati Reds t-shirt and blue jeans. There was no fear in her voice as she addressed Uncle Harold. He simply smiled.

"It's been a long, challenging night and I've paid the highest price, suffered the greatest loss. I will keep this simple; you can work for me or die. I am a strong proponent of fairness and equal compensation." Uncle Harold stared directly at the woman; Giselle James.

She ran the late night after hour establishments that served everything. Although drugs were moved in great quantity from the company she kept, her specialty was information gathering, and Uncle Harold knew she was undervalued by P. Crisp.

"So, what say you?"

"I'll ride wit you." Giselle spoke first followed by an older black man, Irvine Landry, aka IV, because he ran the connection of heroin through the influential neighborhoods of the city.

Uncle Harold nodded his head in agreement to accept them into his organization.

The other two men present hesitated and it cost them their lives as Uncle Harold killed two birds with one stone. He got Giselle and Irvine's loyalty by making them shoot the two others.

"Today, our family empire has taken root."

CHAPTER 1

WELL, SHE IS PRETTY...

Cleveland, Ohio was surprisingly sunny and warm once they hit the outer belt of the city. The drive up I71 didn't seem like it took long with them talking and Kendal practicing his poems out loud. Once they arrived at his parent's home, Kendal was ushered away to help his father with some plumbing at one of their rental properties.

Mattie probably knew just as much as they did about home improvements but Gloria, Kendal's mom, wanted her to stay and help her cook dinner.

Mattie understood completely from Gloria's first comment,

"Hmm, well she is very pretty." That Gloria was sizing her up.

It wasn't necessarily meant as a compliment. What it meant was, 'oh she's pretty but can she take care of my son or have any redeeming qualities.' So, in her own way, Gloria having Mattie all to herself in the kitchen was testing her ability to nourish her son properly, among other things.

"I'm gonna let you cook the green beans. Now you can cook, can't you?" Gloria asked with a slightly pessimistic undertone. Nothing overt, but with just enough negativity that Mattie knew she was hoping Kendal's new pretty girlfriend would not measure up.

Mattie responded by telling her she would make the potato salad, green beans and bake the chicken breasts. She was nervous, but she could cook, she had been taught by her mother and grandmother, and they had been taught by their elders. Mattie knew how to cook soul food, southern foods, a few Native American dishes, Italian, Latino and Asian foods, so she settled down and started boiling a seasoned turkey leg and okra in water for the green beans. By the time she was pulling the chicken out of the oven, Gloria had opened up to her with kindness.

"My son is extremely picky, sometimes too damn picky and I am far worse, but when Doug and Kimberly called and told me about their brother meeting someone, of course I had to know what the fuss was about." She added more marshmallows and pineapples to the candied yams on a lower level in her stove. She took another spoonful of Mattie's potato salad, complimenting her on how damn good it was.

"Thank the Lord you can cook because I was going to talk really bad about you, right to your face. Kendal's my baby and I worry about him. I love him and will accept only the best for him. Are you the best for my son? Time will tell."

They continued making a few more items; rolls and a lemon pound cake while they learned more about each other.

Mattie made gravy for the stuffing, feeling more at ease

and accepted by Kendal's mother.

Gloria explained to Mattie that she had went back out last night to the grocery store after being told that Kendal was bringing her up.

"Normally I would have Doug Sr. take us out to dinner, but you're the only woman he's introduced us to since Janine," Gloria paused as if reflecting.

"Anyway, I needed to spend one on one time with you, thus this whole cooking fiasco. I think I like you Madison."

When Kendal and his dad returned, they got changed and cleaned up before sitting down to eat.

Kendal talked about growing up and how strict his father seemed to be, but as he matured, he saw his dad's strictness as discipline.

Many of his friends in East Cleveland had taken different routes; some successful attorneys or athletes, but a large portion were caught up in the system of survival or being locked away doing time. Kendal reminisced about trying to bully Kim's boyfriends, and she in return calling his girlfriends, acting like she was his girlfriend. Kendal got agitated when his father reminded everyone how Doug

Jr. used to rough him up as kids.

They laughed and joked, and Mattie thought about how his life had been shaped and formed by his parents.

Gloria and Mattie cleared the table after eating, as Kendal and his father sat out on the back wooden deck.

"Your mom likes her, and as good as she can cook, I like her too. It's only been a few months, are you sure you love this woman son?"

His father was at least three inches taller than him, but they shared the same broad shoulders and big hands. He still had a head full of hair, but it was gray, and he looked younger than sixty-five years old. His father chewed on the end of cigar listening to his youngest son.

"Yes sir, I do love her." Kendal had no wavering in his voice.

His father took a sip of cognac and lit his cigar before putting his hand on top of Kendal's.

"Well that's all I need to hear, I'm happy for you. You know after Janine; I felt your loss, your sorrow. It broke my heart. Now it's made you stronger son, turned you into the man you are right now and I'm so very proud of you."

When Janine had passed from cervical cancer, it had taken a toll on Kendal. He watched her wither away but never lost hope until the actual instant she transitioned.

For nearly two years after her death Kendal saw a psychologist to help him sort through it all; which led to him selling the restaurants and moving to San Diego, California for two years and then ending up in Columbus, Ohio.

"Thanks dad, it was rough, but God got me through it and Janine would like her, don't you think?" The question was rhetorical.

"How long are you all staying in town?"

The gray-haired man took another sip of his cognac and began rocking back and forth.

"Eric has a room downtown waiting for us, so we'll be here until the morning. Do you guys wanna get up and go to breakfast?"

Kendal reached over and took the glass out of his father's hand to take a sip.

"Boy don't be getting drunk on my patio." Gloria appeared in the screen door.

"Either of you want coffee with your cake?" She asked with a big smile on her face staring at Kendal.

"Yes, ma'am I do, and why are you smiling like that? Did you do something to Mattie or something?" Kendal stood up and walked back inside, kissing his mother on the cheek as he passed her.

"And thanks dad."

"Kendal, I like her." His mom stepped to the side to let him pass.

Kendal smiled and sat down in the kitchen, while Mattie spread the final bit of glaze on top of the lemon pound cake.

"I love pound cake. Have I ever told you that? Next to carrot cake this is my favorite sweet," he paused to pull her into him.

"Next to that sweet wetness you got that is." Kendal slapped her on her ass.

Mattie shook her head taking another look outside at his parents to make sure they had not seen their son's behavior.

Gloria was sitting on Doug Sr.'s lap in the chair.

"You left me here punk, I was nervous cooking while she caught glances at what I was doing. I almost cooked that chicken too long," she paused and turned around to give him a quick kiss.

"She asked me what I thought about children." She pulled away from him.

They had plenty of conversations up to this point, deep discussions about God and life, as well as in depth talks about love and loss. However, children had never been a topic discussed between them.

"Well, what did you tell her?" Kendal asked staring at her. He wanted kids but Janine had been sick, and he never believed that he would find someone to share his life while raising kids like his mom and dad had. Two loving parents that showed their children what dedication and hard work would bring. As Kendal waited for his answer the coffee machine began spitting out the last bit of water.

"I told her I'd love to have kids as a married woman." Mattie answered in a casual manner, but she wanted to hear him say something about it.

"Baby you won her over just being yourself; you made a perfect impression on both of them." Kendal reached above the kitchen counter for three coffee cups.

"You ever think about how many children you would like?" He asked her, without commenting on what he felt about kids. Mattie wasn't about to reveal her thoughts and be standing on this ledge without knowing what his mind was thinking.

"I never really put a number on it, just imagined the family unit. What about you?" she asked pouring coffee into the mugs.

"Where do they keep the cream honey?"

"Cream is above the microwave, should be at least. I think two to four kids would fit perfectly for us." Kendal answered the question Mattie needed answered.

His parents walked back in from the patio.

"Madison, I am so impressed by the way you

handled yourself with my wife. She had it out for you last night, but you held your own, not something many people can do."

Gloria pushed him playfully in the back.

"Forty-eight years being together, and you still can't handle me." She laughed before bringing up the subject of the trip to North Carolina.

"You're bringing Madison to go meet your brother for the holidays?"

Gloria didn't wait for an answer from her youngest.

"Madison it is so pretty down in Carolina." She added as Kendal handed her a cup of coffee and a piece of Mattie's cake.

"If Kendal Abraham is asking me to go, of course I will, I would love to meet the rest of the family." The sly grin on her face appeared, knowing that he didn't like hearing his middle name.

"We're going to get along just fine I see, the women in your family must be head strong too." Gloria added.

Mattie responded with a simple smile and a nod of her head.

"Well boy it looks like you gonna be just fine, yup just fine." His father showed signs of relief.

"Geez are y'all all trying to gang up on me, we're going to go ahead, get out of here and go see Eric."

"How's he doing, he keeps telling us to come visit his new hotel and he would hook us up, but you know your father, he likes sleeping in his own bed. You know what, have him call me so I can see if we can get a hook up in Charlotte, and you don't have a choice about it big daddy. I want a plush room for that week. Maybe let Kendal and Mattie stay in Juniors' guest house this time for a couple of days and then we can switch." Gloria was visibly happy for her son.

"Oh, I got a choice woman," his father replied, pausing in between watching her raise her eyebrows and taking a bite of her cake.

"But my choice has been, is and will always be you. So, I don't care if we sleep in the Penthouse Suite or a cardboard box, as long as I got you." He finished by kissing her on the lips.

"See that Madison, we don't take no mess." She turned her shoulder so her husband couldn't get the last bit of her cake.

Kendal was happy because his parents had taken to Mattie, she was becoming an extended member of Kendal's family in just one day.

"Anyways, do you all want to meet for breakfast, IHOP or somewhere?" Kendal asked before following up with another,

"...and are you all coming down to Columbus or Cincinnati before next month's trip. The kids keep asking about when you both are coming back."

"We might come spend a few days before hand to stay with you, if you're up to it. Madison maybe you, I and your grandmother could have lunch. She sounds like a wonderful, intelligent elder. I don't want no IHOP, lord no. We'll talk about it later, but I'm sure Madison is exhausted from cooking, along with me running her through the ringer today. When we go down South, we're shopping for two days." His mom finished as Kendal wrapped aluminum foil around a large container holding food in it.

"We'll see you tomorrow and I'll give Eric your cell phone number."

His parents hugged Mattie and then gave him a hug.

"Kendal, you better take care of this one." Gloria whispered in her son's ear, but Mattie heard her while pretending not to be paying attention.

"I will mom, you don't have to even worry about it." Kendal walked out the front door, holding it for Mattie with a big smile on his face.

"Mr. and Mrs. Scott, it was my pleasure meeting you, thank you so much for having me in your house, in your kitchen." She said light-heartedly as she gave Gloria a farewell hug.

"Ok now, we'll see you all tomorrow."

Kendal's father watched Kendal open Mattie's door and kiss her on the cheek.

"She reminds me of you, when we were younger. God has a funny way of rewarding us." He waved one final time.

"Yeah baby ain't that the truth."

CHAPTER 2

EAST CLEVELAND

Kendal's friend, Eric, managed a five-star hotel with recently upgraded Penthouse Suites. Mattie and Kendal ended up staying in one of those rooms, with vaulted ceilings and concrete marble floors.

The sitting area was directly in the middle of the room with white, leather, long-tufted upholstered benches placed between open arch ways. Towards the end of the main room extended a large glass pane, opening to a sky balcony which overlooked Lake Erie.

A small stone pit had already been lit prior to their arrival. The wind blew the flames back and forth contrasting against the night sky.

Mattie had Kendal make love to her under the stars on the balcony that night. It was the first night that they had expressed their love for each other verbally and now they couldn't be separated.

Mattie decided to take the next two days off. Cleveland had been fabulous and memorable; she had made a good impression on Kendal's parents and she liked them too.

She told Cindy and Geri about it Tuesday morning while she lay in bed and Kendal explained to his parents that 'he' woke up late, so they missed breakfast.

Mattie also told her friends about Kendal's upcoming performance with Kwame, bringing people to the show at Café Coffee Bean. Geri confirmed she would be there for support; Cindy had a prior engagement.

Tuesday was a blur after their return.

Kendal was tied up in meetings and taking over one of the adult classes.

Mattie forced herself to the MMA gym and found herself teaching a class on striking, with Jennifer being short staffed. She headed to the park later that evening, running with the group she had before.

Mattie drove to the poetry venue so that Kendal could focus strictly on his performance after ripping and running around all day. He had overbooked appointments and meetings with both parents and other community leaders on what programs were suited best to help those in need.

Kendal proposed running a food pantry once a month out of the center; while a few district representatives spoke about paying tutors to help public school students in mathematics and science. With more hands stirring the pot, Kendal tried being as diplomatic as possible to ensure progress would be made.

When the meeting ran an hour longer than planned, he asked to table the conversations until later. The break was needed before real disagreement came to the front and he needed time to exhale before the performance.

The crowd was eclectic, a cross cultural representation of the community. The coffee shop made additional space to accommodate fifty more seats.

Mattie was grateful that Geri showed up on time as the show started.

The poets performing tonight were all more seasoned than the artists who performed at Da Island the night Kwame hosted, and it was noticeable. Kendal said he wasn't nervous, but his palms were sweaty.

A national promoter and sponsor had accompanied Kwame just like he had said, and they had already selected artists for the tour, but Kwame had made them promise to come out and listen to Kendal to give him a chance. Although he wasn't nationally known, Kwame had faith in him because he knew talent when he saw it.

Kendal wanted this badly, he had woken up Tuesday morning going over each line of the poem to get the cadence down, and that was one of the reasons they hadn't made breakfast with his parents, plus he had been in full appreciation of Mattie's nakedness.

Mattie was clapping her hands as the first poet finished her poem. It was a heartfelt piece about having a miscarriage that touched both Geri and Mattie. Mattie sat with a little worry, but Geri reinforced that Kendal would do just fine as he walked up on the platform.

Café Coffee Bean was vastly different than Da Island. Da Island for all intents and purposes was a night club that offered a poetry night. Café Coffee Bean was a coffee shop on one side, separated with a room to hold roughly sixty people on the other. Espressos were the strongest concoction under this roof, although on some nights they added 'spirits' to specialty drinks.

Mattie had done research on the establishment and found out that it had hosted international spoken word events, with people traveling from across the globe to participate. The last national spoken word artist had frequented the coffee shop and was spreading through word of mouth about how great of a place it was.

The artists performing tonight were by invitation only. They had traveled from Georgia, Michigan, and even Virginia. Kendal wrote a fictional piece that was based on his friends' life growing up in East Cleveland. His delivery kept everyone listening for nearly five minutes.

"I want you to pretend that make believe didn't exist, so that the best chance to get acclimated to life is to know that death is just the flip-side of your first breath and those in between moments, when air

was first passing into your lungs, is probably the
same exhale of oxygen that was released prior to
our great grand folks being hung. I wasn't sprung
in the Springtime, but I was the first born with no
cheddar; so, I had to wait in the ghetto cheese line.
You know my willie bobo's was hand me downs and
that was passed down after the third time.

So, as I watched my older cousins exert their
muscle game it helped me realize that my hood, my
family had one of the betta hustle games. My uncle
played at politics and one aunt taught. With the
shame of holes in my Chuck Taylors and
socks it made me grow up faster by introducing me
to the school of hard knocks, my pro-jected idea of
my projects, should've been to pro-tect those who
needed it, instead I banged dope and weed and the
pretty girls wearing weaves and shit. I was just
thirteen years old and was already learning how to
be phenomenal, whether in baseline to baseline
dribbles or in one hundred-yard bursts. Impossible
at the time to know the thirst in my grind, refined
ten dollars into three holla's and I kept dimes
dropping on the court. Regardless of the game I

kept studying the intricate details of the sport. I saw that loud cats got the attention, but they also got played, so I moved in the shadows real quiet like and got myself paid. First little click was American Gigolo. First gang EC Brick City Outlaw; and it was one of the first times when I got acquainted with a toolie, was about twenty minutes before I ran into a couple of Italiano's and then got called mulee.

So, with the thought of squeezing the burner, you know that thirty-eight that was tucked by my hip, I made a decision to knuckle up with two grown ass men and afterwards one of em learned the value of a teenagers tre eight pistol whip. Never personal always business, so with my relentless pursuit to know the difference I almost got shot, but instead my cat playing Russian Roulette took the chance first and the lead dumped into his head was hot. Many say that life can change in the blink of an eye, but for me it was changed with the click of a finger, self-induced senseless death had me shook, 'cause I was ready to ride or die for my nucka. I remember explaining that I don't eat pork

or talk to pigs so with his parents crying about their
son dying cause apparently it was he who split his
own wig. *My credentials gained ground and I got to
chill with the old gangsta's, indoctrinated into the
life, mo cheese, I learned the OG's first and final
statement was 'make me rich but don't make me
famous.' Six packs were my product but like
BG's I had to start with a teenager, I took that one
point seven five and merchandised it into six G
packs it was the beginning of stacking paper.*

*Some of my, competition got knocked, so with
those many blocks remaining vacant, I devised a
plan for increasing the foundation for my own
corporate takin. I slapped box with some of my
partners just to see who had heart, a few with the
heavy hands I paid for any man who tried to forget
to pay for their part. Getting shit off
at nighttime, Glenville Park, right after dark. Right
after I sparked spin moves for the Academes, the
same squad that my father balled with, I had two
other dads in my life, and I bet some of
y'all would think that's some odd shit. One was my
seed bearer because from the best of my*

recollection I was just a seed when he planned the set-up, rob the bar with his homie get the loot then get to steppin. Now for armed robbery I think you get seven for a weapon but my dad, the seed bearer, shot and took the last breath before the called the victim a murdered dead man. A twenty plus bit so mom had to spit me out alone went for visits behind bars where hardened men found religion. My dad found Islam, me and mom Jehovah's witness, and me seven years old was my first spoken word, as mom got married, I became one of the Smiths'.

Now son of an electrician who worked for Cleveland's cardiac kids, a good man but who had issues, mom used rolls of paper towels instead of boxes of tissue. Strangled hands were the deterrent. One day there, next day we weren't. Life moved on parallel to mainstream but I was still caught in the torrent of the ghetto current. The garden valley I knew wasn't filled with rows of carrots, greens or tomatoes. Instead exchange the shit with addicts, fiends and imported hoes. The working girls would shout out 'twenty make you holla' but then twenty girls went dead. East side of

*Cleveland, but specifically, I am an East Cleveland
product. I learned to shoot a BB rifle before I got
my miles up. As I aged my style got kinda eclectic,
rustic like Jimi Hendrix or a present-day Jill Scott,
I've watched old men OD off heroin trying to make
it to heaven like Gil Scott. My mind is fragmented
from all the jagged edges and muted ledges, I'm not
sure what else my mind will dredge up from the
pressure of putting pieces back to my broken
mirror.*

The promoter and sponsor loved it and offered him a slot
to tour with them; they would need his commitment within
the month to add him to the promotional advertisements.

They provided him with the schedule of dates and cities
they were booked in already, with other cities trying to
schedule. Along with the schedule they gave Kendal a few
CD's of the other artists work.

"Kendal, Kwame told us about you initially when we
pushed the idea around. Our main priority was to get only
nationally recognized artists with a following, which we
have accomplished for the most part." Stephen Blue, the
promoter was a short man, about five feet five inches tall

with curly red hair. He wore a goatee and rimless glasses. What stood out was the diamond necklace around his neck in the shape of a cross. His navy-blue dress slacks and cream-colored cotton button down shirt reminded Mattie and Geri of Tom Cruise's role in Tropic Thunder.

The other person was a woman who looked to be in her mid- fifties. She dressed fashionably and had a slender build; the lines of her body were proportioned. Her movements were graceful, and she had presence. Even with wrinkles and small bags under her eyes, by any standard she was a beautiful woman.

"They had to drag me here because my mind was already set. I wasn't taking anyone else, even after watching your performance on the DVD. I thought that piece was awesome, but I thought you were playing to the crowd and it was a poem already written down and memorized. Now I realize it was spur of the moment and you are as talented, if not more, than some of the one's we've selected already."

Patricia Byrne was the investor of the project, having her blessing to join a legendary mix of spoken word artists meant a lot. Some had performed in front of previous

Presidents and all had Best Sellers on all the major lists.

"I love that blouse." Patricia added touching Mattie's sleeve.

"Well, I'm glad they made you come out tonight and that you're more flexible than what Kwame had led me to believe Patricia." Kendal said squeezing Mattie's hand.

Kwame and Patricia were intimate, and intimate may have been too personal, they were more like sex partners. Patricia wanted more, but Kwame made her play her role and she understood how to compartmentalize the business and the personal.

"Yes, I can be stubborn at times. With this tour being my baby, I am only accepting the best performing artists, so I have to stretch myself a little more than I want sometimes, and you both can call me Pat." She winked at Mattie.

Mattie found it slightly odd and Geri caught the wink as she came back from getting an iced mocha.

"Patricia Byrne, Stephen Blue, this is Geri Marcom." Kwame licked his bottom lip.

"You look familiar, where have I seen you before?"

Patricia was curious until the light bulb went off in her head.

"You're on the DVD, the same one Kendal was on, that's right. Your poem stood out along with Kendal's. You know when we come back to Columbus, maybe you would like to join your fellow thespians on the stage."

"As much as I enjoyed that night, my skills are nowhere near these, and I'm ok with that. Plus, I'll have major deadlines and scheduling interviews I'll be worrying about," but Stephen interrupted.

"What type of work do you do business wise? You said schedule interviews?" He was a businessman, quick on his feet and always looking for opportunities.

"I'm owner, co- publisher and editor for "Under the Sun" we're predominantly in the Midwest market up until recently. We just added a few more distribution channels on the east coast and down in Florida and Georgia. We'd love to interview you and maybe a few of the artists you have locked down already for the tour. It would be a great way to introduce the tour and we'd have an opportunity to be in the 'know and the now'. Geri handed her business cards to both as her phone started vibrating.

Mattie was checking her phone too as it vibrated in her purse. Sheila had called her twice and left a voice message.

Geri excused herself to answer her phone.

"Hey girl what's up?"

It was Sheila.

"What!" Geri was instantly agitated with concern on her face.

"Oh my God, we're on the way, she's right here with me." Geri said frantically.

Mattie was listening to Kwame tell Patricia that Columbus was overflowing with talent and that scheduling an extra show might prove rewarding when Geri grabbed her arm.

"We have to get to the hospital right now, Sheila just called." Geri pulled Mattie away.

"What's up, is she ok?" Mattie attempted to ask but Geri told everyone she was taking Mattie with her and demanded Kendal to follow them in Mattie's car.

CHAPTER 3

WHO IS THAT MS. REDD?

Grandma Redd had fallen asleep in her recliner chair in the bedroom after being outside on the patio taking care of the garden. The day had been decently warm for late fall; which in turn drained energy from her. She loved being in the sun, but now she could only tolerate an hour here and there without feeling the effects of it.

Her intentions were to go back out and finish what she had started when the sun went down, but she ended up more exhausted than expected. She opened her eyes hearing something in the kitchen break, so she stood up pulling her oxygen tank with her.

Maybe she had misread Kendal and now Mattie was home having difficulty with her emotions again, like she had when her parents had been taken away. Grandma Redd knew just how strong Mattie had become, but she was aware of how fragile her granddaughter was emotionally at times.

She walked across the hardwood floors in her slippers and the sound of cabinets being swung open, followed by dishes falling to the floor had her worried. Mattie hadn't had temper tantrums since she began seeing her psychologist as a teen over a decade ago.

"Oh Lord, Kendal has pissed her off." She opened her bedroom door. The lights in the living room and kitchen were still off, which was unlike Mattie who didn't like fumbling around in the dark, and that's when Grandma Redd felt something wasn't right hearing a male's voice that wasn't Kendal's.

"Fuck." Was all she heard.

She heard footsteps in the kitchen, and the skylight cast a shadow of the intruder into the living room as he moved around. Grandma Redd made it back into her bedroom and closed the door. Her cell phone was on the TV tray; she picked it up and dialed 911.

"911 emergency, how may I help you?" the operator asked.

"Someone broke into the house, the address is," Grandma Redd led with information. Mattie told her to give the address first when calling from a cell phone because a wireless signal was carried from a cell phone tower and the address didn't always populate.

"Ma'am are they still there? Are you safe? I have officers in route, ma'am…ma'am." The operator repeated lowly.

Grandma Redd didn't answer because she heard tennis shoes squeaking down the hallway wood floor.

"They're coming to my door."

Grandma Redd tried whispering into the receiver, but when the door to her bedroom was jiggled and opened, she screamed with all she could muster.

"Get out my house, I'm on the phone with the police!" She yelled standing her ground because it was all she could do at this point.

"Hold on ma'am, they're in route." The operator said loudly hoping the intruder heard her.

"Give me that fucking phone old bitch, where's the fucking money and jewelry, I ain't fucking with your old ass." A husky voice said before the operator heard the phone being smashed against a wall.

He was a bit panicked now knowing someone was home and the police on their way, so he grabbed Grandma Redd and started shaking her.

She dug her nails into his arms before trying to scratch him to fight back, but he was too young and too strong.

He punched her and then pushed her up against her wooded hutch. She bounced off it and fell to the ground, before he kicked her in the side.

"You shoulda jus told me where it was." He said, pulling out her jewelry box and finding the hidden stash of money. She had diamond earrings and tennis bracelets;

Mattie's mother's wedding ring, along with her father's diamond bracelet. There was nearly ten thousand dollars' worth of jewelry and another eighteen hundred dollars in cash that he was making off with.

Grandma Redd lay on the floor feeling something warm run down the back of her neck. She struggled to breathe, she fought to stand up, but she couldn't think coherently. She wanted to do more, but right now she was praying to God and hoping that this ordeal was almost over. She could hear the police car sirens as the intruder ran back down the hall and out of the house, the same way he had gotten in.

The police were buzzed into the building by a tenant, before kicking the front door down to Mattie's unit. They found Grandma Redd lying at the bathroom door trying to prop herself up. She was wheezing, and blood was dripping down her neck from a deep head abrasion. The paramedics tried stopping the bleeding as she faded in and out of consciousness; she only caught glimpses of being wheeled into the ambulance and then into the emergency room of the hospital.

"Ma'am can you tell us your name, is there anyone you want us to call?"

Grandma Redd heard people talking to her as she laid on a bed in the emergency room. Doctors were barking orders on what to be done first, but she couldn't make out any faces because one of her eyes was swollen shut and the other one, she couldn't focus.

"Madison." She said softly.

"Who is that Ms. Redd, who would you like us to call?"

"Madison." She repeated before passing out on the bed in the emergency room.

CHAPTER 4

FAMILY IS MOST IMPORTANT

The hospital was normally a twenty-minute drive away, but Geri barely stopped for lights and cut people off, they arrived in about half that time. She hadn't said a word to Mattie, who sat still in the passenger seat holding onto the strap of her seat belt. Geri almost hit a couple of people being wheeled out of the hospital.

Sheila was waiting for them at the valet parking booth when they pulled up. The wetness on her cheeks indicated she had been crying.

"What's wrong, you guys are scaring me?" Mattie asked, as Kendal pulled up behind them. He had got caught at the light before turning in to the emergency room oval.

"They broke into your house Mattie, they hurt grandma…they hurt her, she's in the operating room right now. The doctors are relieving pressure built up on her brain. Two ribs are fractured but no broken bones." Sheila took Mattie by the hand leading her past the emergency room check-in desk.

The yellow walls and the cold sterile environment had no calming effect on Mattie's nerves, as they moved with haste through the corridors. She had not been home to protect her grandmother.

"Where is she?" Mattie asked, as Sheila led them into an office in the surgery wing.

"They've got the best doctors attending to her; I didn't take no shit from any of them. I told them that she was my grandmother and to treat her like the fucking president. I'm going right now to get an update." Sheila walked out of the glass doors of the office, pushing past those attending other patients.

A police officer with a clipboard in his hands was speaking with a nurse as Mattie watched Sheila walk up interrupting them. Sheila was asking the nurse about the status of the surgery when Mattie came busting through the door.

"I gotta see her Lala, I gotta see her." Mattie just didn't know where to go.

"She will be coming out of surgery soon, but its gonna take time. I'll go back and check but just wait. Talk with Nurse Galloway, and the policeman has the report." Sheila urged Mattie to wait.

"Ms. Parks." The officer interjected, as Kendal and Geri accompanied Mattie who was listening attentively.

"If we can step back into the office, I'll give you what I have, and I'll need to ask you a few questions." He was a younger white man with dark brown hair, clean shaven and thin.

"Come on baby, Sheila will be back, and he can tell us what happened." Kendal put his arm around her as support when Cindy burst through the double doors running down the hall.

Mattie looked dazed and confused as she sat down on the couch in the office. The officer told Mattie they had received a 911 call at 9:13 pm and that officers arrived at 9:19. He advised that the patio door was opened, and it didn't look like forced entry. They found Grandma Redd bleeding from her head and semi-conscious. She had trauma to her face with deep bruising in her back.

Nurse Galloway interrupted them to share that the surgery had went well, and the surgeon had taken care of the immediate concern of swelling in the brain, which helped stabilize Grandma Redd's blood pressure, and now she was in the recovery room.

Mattie got sick and threw up in the waste basket, so Nurse Galloway got her some ice chips to help keep her hydrated. The officer asked Mattie what time she had left that evening and if she knew anyone that may have wanted to harm her or her grandmother. He recognized that right now the family was in pain. He asked a few more routine questions before excusing himself to let them cope.

Sheila came back in to verify everything Nurse Galloway had said. The only difference in Sheila's report was that Grandma Redd was in a coma and she still had fluid in her lungs. She was being moved and monitored into the Intensive Care Unit. Sheila ensured that the elder woman had a private room with access to a secondary room close by for family.

The first day was touch and go with her blood pressure fluctuating. Once it was stabilized her vitals got better each day after, although she remained in a coma.

Mattie never left her side and Kendal remained with her, supporting Mattie every second of every minute. Geri and Sheila only left a few hours both days, but they were also spending much of their time with Mattie in the hospital.

Cindy made sure that she was there every morning to watch The Price is Right and soap operas on TV; the ones Grandma Redd enjoyed most.

Sheila brought food in at the beginning of her shifts. She kept it simple; peanut butter and jelly sandwiches; turkey and cheese sandwiches with BBQ chips and she had dinner delivered at night.

Henry and Michelle paid their respect, and it was Michelle who offered to keep Darian and Samantha a few days with them, she would ensure school and everything else stayed on track. Henry kept the family updated on what little information they had. The initial report indicated what they already knew, breaking and entering through the patio door.

Mattie needed to make a list of items missing so he could add it to the report whenever she returned home.

The elder woman was intubated along with two smaller clear tubes going into both of her nostrils. The IV in her right arm provided nutrients and medicine that her body desperately needed. Mattie finally dozed off on the third night as Cindy and Geri slept on the couch in the family space.

Kendal had his laptop and notebook on the desk, working while he remained by Mattie's side. He understood the power of prayer, so he prayed. In a little more than three months, he had grown a bond with Grandma Redd and was feeling Mattie's pain.

Flowers, balloons and cards poured in for Grandma Redd, some of the flowers were on the nurse's station and more were given to other patients who didn't have any loved ones to support them. Sheila allowed Mattie and Kendal to use the hospital showers, because they weren't leaving until

Grandma Redd came out of the coma and got better. Mattie was forming a deeper bond with Kendal as she relied on him, this vulnerability was also intimate.

The swelling in Grandma's face had gone down after the third day in the hospital bed. Her lips were still bruised, but healing. Sheila had a nurse check on her every couple of hours to make sure the bruising on her back had not worsened.

The sun was shining in between the mini-blinds onto the floor at the base of her hospital bed starting the fourth day. The glowing radiance created a pattern across the tiled floor.

Kendal walked in, sliding the glass door open that separated both rooms. He had gone down to the cafeteria to get coffee and now returned with four mugs in a Styrofoam carrier for everyone.

He saw the slight body movement before making eye contact with Grandma Redd who tried to say something. Kendal's eyebrows heightened while he motioned for the elder woman not to attempt to speak.

Her eyes traveled to Madison sitting in the chair with her

head leaning onto the bed railing.

"No grandma, you can't talk right now." Kendal's voice stirred Mattie awake.

"Grandma." She leaned upward and moved closer to say something.

"Grandma I'm so sorry, I love you." she started to show her emotions again.

Grandma Redd was realizing what had happened. She was in pain but alive. She tried to shake her head at Mattie not to cry, and then she did something unexpectedly.

The elder woman took Mattie's hand and put it on top of Kendal's before putting hers on top of Mattie's, all while staring Mattie in her eyes so she would understand the message.

She approved of Kendal for her granddaughter; he was the only man to receive her approval, her blessing.

Kendal wasn't sure if he completely understood, but he kept his hand fixated on the bed rail with Mattie and her grandmother's holding his hand down.

Geri and Cindy were waking up as the nurse followed the two attending physicians into the room. After running additional tests and checking the results, they pulled the tubes from the elder woman's throat, but the oxygen mask remained, preventing her from talking much.

For the first time in four days Mattie was dealing with an emotion other than sadness, she was angry at whoever did this and if she ever found out who they were, she was going to punish them, and no one would be able to talk her out of it.

The doctor asked Mattie to go home and rest. Grandma Redd was out of the woods for the most part, the major concern now was monitoring her ribs, as two had been fractured during the assault. The elder woman scribbled on a piece of paper 'GO' for Mattie to leave, indicating she was fine. Nurse Galloway wrote down both Mattie and Kendal's cell phone numbers to call in case of an emergency. Mattie reluctantly left, making Kendal drive her home, the first time she would be walking through the door after the burglary.

The yellow police tape had been taken down already as they walked through the door for the first time in days.

Cindy and Geri had gone over the previous day and cleaned up the mess, so it was less of an emotional onslaught when she arrived back home.

They had scrubbed the floor to get the blood up, growing angry and sad in those same moments. Imagining how someone had injured a woman they both deeply adored.

"Honey I can grab your clothes and we can go to my place if you're overwhelmed."

Kendal felt Mattie squeeze his hand walking through the front door. Nothing seemed out of place and the first thing Mattie did was walk to the patio door to make sure it was locked.

"I'm ok, it's better for me to deal with the emotions now rather than later, just don't leave me...don't ever leave me. We will sleep at your place tonight." She took his hand to walk back to her grandmother's room, each step made her queasy approaching the door.

Kendal pushed it all the way open.

Mattie let out a sigh. She was expecting the room to be a mess, but the bed was made, and the floors scrubbed spotless.

"Those women did a good job." Mattie said out loud.

She walked to the hutch to take inventory of what was missing so she could give the description to the police. Luckily, there were tissue samples collected from under Grandma Redd's nails, but, so far, no suspect profile had been generated.

"You want something to write on, I'll grab something from the office." Kendal walked out of the bedroom and into the next room.

Right away, she noticed that the cash was gone, along with the jewelry box. The box had both her grandmother's and mother's jewelry in it. Wedding rings and charms among other trinkets.

Her father's ring and bracelet were gone too. His bracelet was made overseas as a reminder of what he and his friends had gone through in the military.

It was an expensive bracelet with a very distinctive weave to it and seven diamonds spread across it, to match the bond he shared with six other men. The value of it - priceless.

Kendal walked back into the room with a notepad and ink

pen.

"Thank you, will you pack some clothes in the bag we took to Cleveland. I'll shower at your house. I just feel sick, do you mind?"

"Honey my house is your house; you don't have to ask me that. I'll throw a couple pairs of jeans, sweats and tops in it." He knew how important it was to support Mattie in any capacity required, he would even support her if she was in the wrong. Kendal loved her completely and without condition.

Mattie was walking back into her room with the list in her hand. She would fax it into the police from Kendal's condo, and later she would have to make another list for the insurance company.

"Let me put some more stuff in there just in case Grandma doesn't get out for another week or so. I'll stay with you until she comes home." Mattie found a positive thought to hold onto. Returning home with her grandmother was a silver lining among these tumultuous times.

She could feel the power of wanting vengeance rise

inside for the person responsible for violating her Grandmother and her home.

"Family is most important." Mattie said out loud as she added a jogging suit, sweatpants and another pair of jeans to the bag. She grabbed more panties and some toiletries from her bathroom.

A bag sticking out from beneath her bed caught his attention, he bent down to pick it up and noticed 'adult' items. He took his foot and pushed it further under the bed.

"Anything else you need honey?"

Kendal watched her from the bathroom entrance.

Mattie was near the bathroom counter with watery eyes. She leaned over the counter to stare into the mirror.

"If I ever find out who did this, I'm going to hurt them, bad." She stared into the mirror back towards Kendal, who stood in the archway between her bedroom and bathroom.

She had a blank expression on her face and appeared composed, but beneath she seethed with anger and pain.

"I understand." He met her eyes.

Kendal recognized the look, because it was the same emotion he carried watching his departed wife Janine transition, but his enemy was cancer and he had no viable way to seek retribution.

Mattie would serve her own justice if the opportunity presented itself, and she wanted Kendal to know how serious she was right now.

"Baby I mean every word I say, if I find out who did it, I'll have to ask God for forgiveness this time." She didn't blink.

"I understand,' he repeated.

Mattie checked all the windows in the house to make sure they were locked, and she went back into the dining room to check the patio door again.

"Honey will you set the alarm?" Mattie motioned to her alarm pad, as she checked her gun carrier to put into one of her bags.

"You think you need it?" Kendal asked.

He didn't care if she brought it, she was sorting through a ton of emotions. He wouldn't push because he knew what was needed was simple support.

"I don't know if I'll need it until I need it." She answered him flatly while checking to make sure she had a box of ammunition and three extra magazines.

"Fair enough, the code is 4567?"

"4567." Mattie confirmed. She had made it as simple as possible so that Grandma Redd could remember.

'But it only works if you set it grandma.'

Mattie thought back to all the times she had uttered those very words, but it wasn't her grandmother's fault, it was the people who broke into her home.

Kendal took an easy route to his home that steered away from congested traffic. Mattie was on the phone speaking with some of her older family members, updating them on Grandma Redd's condition.

Mattie had other relatives; cousins and aunts her age, but most of them lived in the south, so she scarcely remembered them all. A few members wanted to come immediately to Columbus, but Mattie asked them to hold off until Grandma Redd was released from the hospital.

Her Gran Aunt Penny *told* Mattie that she was coming, and she'd be in Columbus by Tuesday afternoon and she needed to be picked up from the airport.

Aunt Penny had the same stubborn streak Mattie possessed, the only difference, Aunt Penny was forty-years Mattie's senior. In the end Mattie had no other option but to agree with her elder's request.

Kendal made Mattie take a quick shower and change while he cleared out two drawers to put her clothes in both. He put the gun case on the nightstand before they left for the hospital to spend time with her recovering elder.

Sheila was already off work when they walked back into the hospital room, she was sitting with Grandma Redd who still wore the oxygen mask.

Grandma's eyes lit up when she saw Mattie and Kendal walk in together.

Kendal bent down and kissed her on her forehead.

Mattie waited until he moved back to hug and kiss her, so she wouldn't be cramping the space surrounding the hospital bed.

"Geri just left, she had to catch up on some work, a deadline is coming up or something with the next edition."

Sheila relinquished the chair so Mattie could sit down next to her grandmother. It appeared that Grandma Redd was trying to smile beneath her mask.

"I'm going to go pick up the kids and bring them back for a quick second, if that's alright with you?" Sheila paused to pull her shoulder bag over her arm.

"They've been praying like crazy for her and for you." She finished.

"I guess that's ok, we just can't let them get Grandma all excited and stuff. I don't know what we would've done without you, the whole staff. Tell them I said thank you, that we thank them for all their care." Mattie stood up to give Sheila a hug.

Holding onto her friend, she was grateful that Sheila ensured Grandma Redd's comfortability during her recovery.

"Come on girl, we're family, my sister. Now stop squeezing me so damn hard." Sheila laughed and held the embrace a little longer.

"Sheila, you need me to carry anything out to your minivan?" Kendal asked with his hand still resting on the bedrail.

He had left the center in the hands of the staff and told Kwame he hadn't decided yet about the tour. Kendal wanted this opportunity to travel with well-known artists to help promote their craft, but he had lived without love and he would sacrifice the tour if staying to support Mattie was required for her well-being. It wasn't a question for him.

"No, I'm good, let me leave so I can get back with the kids." Sheila skirted past Kendal to kiss Grandma Redd.

"I love you grandma."

Grandma Redd shook her head affirmatively to acknowledge Sheila before she left.

Kendal and Mattie realized how tired they were. Kendal let Mattie lay her head on his lap as he sat back on the couch, stroking her hair. A new nurse came to check on Grandma Redd's vitals before smiling at Kendal on the way out.

In a sense this was strengthening him, as he had to deal with his own demons haunting him. He remembered spending countless hours and days at Janine's side, watching her fight with every bit of energy going through chemotherapy; having a relapse and using her courage to forge forward through additional treatment. Kendal never left her side until Janine took her last breath, whispering in his ear that she loved him and to find happiness at her moment of passing.

He bent forward and kissed Mattie before sitting back to fall asleep.

The sound of the door opening stirred them. The time had passed quickly.

Samantha and Darian were busting through the sliding glass door of the hospital room before Sheila had a chance to stop them.

"Wait, wait…wait, she might be sleeping." Sheila said grabbing Samantha by the hand. Darian looked hesitant to approach Grandma Redd's bed seeing her face covered with the oxygen mask and her bed surrounded by monitors.

Their senior was already awake, and her eyes shown the smile that she was unable to display. Sheila walked them by hand to the bed. The children's enthusiasm had subsided slightly, they were now beginning to understand what it meant that she had been harmed.

"Grandma can't talk right now, but she knows you guys are here."

Mattie moved her head off Kendal's lap before adjusting her body to stand and move toward the bed to stand directly behind them.

"Auntie, grandma is gon be ok, right?" Darian asked looking at the bruises on Grandma Redd's face.

"Of course, she's gonna be fine. Grandma is a strong person," Mattie answered, pausing to whisper into Sheila's ear.

"Thank you."

"It's ok, don't go doing that. She's my grandmother and we're sister's, right? We're family and we're stuck with each other for the rest of our lives, thick like molasses." Sheila put her arm around Mattie.

"Baby I have to call the center; Frances should still be there, but the proposals for the grants have to be postmarked by tomorrow."

Kendal excused himself, kissing her cheek before departing.

Mattie walked to the opposite side where she could stand closer to the bed.

Sheila removed the kids into the family room that they had occupied as Grandma Redd recovered. She turned the television on to Teen Titans for Samantha and gave Darian her cell phone to play games.

"The doctor says her vitals are improving but she's still very concerned about her lungs. She hasn't been responding to the treatment as well as expected. It may require follow up examinations to see if some other course of action may work better. Doctor Prishnev will be here first thing in the morning to talk to you." Sheila waited to give Mattie that information after getting her children situated. Kendal re-entered the room as Mattie was responding.

"So, everything is fine except that?"

She would've loved to have been able to say 'so everything is fine' but Mattie saw the extent of the trauma and knew it was going to take time for the tissue and muscles to heal; the fractured ribs even longer.

"Yeah, pretty much, she's been fighting off an infection, but with all the antibiotics we've been pumping, her vitals have been getting stronger. I'm going to take the kids home and let them sleep in their own beds tonight. Plus, I gotta pack their clothes for the weekend. James is supposed to be taking them camping and fishing, we'll see how that goes, call me for anything." She held Grandma Redd's hands while she talked to Mattie.

"I'll call you when we leave, we may stop by before heading back to Kendal's tonight." Mattie paused to hug Darian and Samantha.

"I love you and grandma loves you." Mattie lifted Samantha up to say goodbye.

"Bye grandma, get better and I love you." Samantha said leaning over the rail to kiss the elder woman's cheek.

Darian didn't want help even though he was barley tall enough to lean over the bed rail. He stepped onto his tip toes.

"Grandma I love you too."

"Baby do you mind if I give Lala your cell and home number?" Mattie felt she knew the answer but didn't want to assume.

Kendal was on his phone texting his parents about Grandma Redd's condition after his call with Frances.

His parents were going to drive down the first night they found out she had been injured, but Mattie told Kendal to have them wait. It wasn't that she didn't like the support, but she felt fragile initially.

"Baby that's fine, whatever you need." Kendal answered reading a text message sent back from his mother.

"Mom and dad are still in prayer baby; mom said that if you need anything at all, anything she's here." Kendal finished by telling Sheila's kids that they were very brave and if it was ok with Sheila, he could take everyone for ice cream once Grandma Redd was back home and felt up to it.

She had been around Kendal long enough to know he was a good role model and would protect her children like they were his own. She ushered Samantha and Darian out the door as they all waved goodbye.

A nurse and doctor came in to check the monitors,

ensuring Grandma Redd's breathing was consistent before
removing the oxygen mask. Her lips dry, Mattie reached
into her purse and pulled out a small tube of lip balm. She
tenderly spread it across Grandma Redd's lips before
pouring a little ice into a glass of water to let her
grandmother sip ever so slowly.

"Thank you, Madison." She spoke gingerly, still slightly
feeling the effects of the tubes which had irritated her
throat.

"We're going to get you home as soon as we can."

Mattie wondered what else she could do to make her
more comfortable. There were additional pillows on the
couch, but Grandma Redd shook her head back and forth
knowing what her granddaughter was thinking.

The silver haired woman motioned for Kendal to come
closer, her eyes had wisdom in them as she began to speak.

"You two must take care of each other, you are meant to
be…to be together, commitment."

Mattie took Kendal's hand.

"You have my blessing." It was a completely unexpected

moment and Mattie didn't know how to really take it all in.

"She is assuming I'd say yes?" She thought before answering her own question.

"Of course, I would, but he will have to wait to ask her properly.

"I am tired baby, let me rest. I love you both and you are my heart Madison." She finished by reaching out for Madison again.

"I love you too grandma, we'll be in the room not even twenty feet away, we're right here."

Mattie began walking towards the glass pane to exit.

"Baby." Kendal called out to Mattie, as the elder woman motioned Mattie back towards her bed.

"Madison go home honey, I'm gonna sleep for a while. I love you."

Mattie didn't quite understand why she was being sent away. She felt like a child being told to go to bed by her parents, but she was going to respect her request.

"Yes ma'am, Aunt Penny will be here in a couple of

days, so I'll clean up the guest room for her. I don't want to leave you here by yourself." Mattie responded, reluctant to leave the hospital.

"We can leave in the morning Grandma."

Grandma Redd made her leave with Kendal. She knew her granddaughter would exhaust every bit of energy for her and from the look of it, Mattie had none left. Mattie needed to eat and really sleep. Knowing her elder was coherent and speaking she felt better, as she and Kendal walked out of the Intensive Care Unit.

CHAPTER 5

UNTIL TOMORROW

Knowing her grandmother could communicate now, Mattie found moments to exhale. They were still giving Grandma Redd nutrients through her IV, but she had slowly been given a little broth throughout the day. Even with the improvements, Mattie and Kendal spent most of their hours at the hospital.

The hospital staff had been highly attentive, Mattie

attributed it to the type of respect Sheila had inside these walls. Mattie's trust in the staff allowed her to leave the hospital when she got hungry or tired. She and Kendal decided to head out for some food. They made small pleasantries with the staff as they passed the nursing station, but Mattie was even hungrier than she was tired, so they kept the exchange short.

The sudden change in temperature had penetrated inside the parking garage and it hit them as soon as they stepped off the elevator heading to his Audi.

Kendal had his arm around Mattie, lending her support. Demons from his past attempted to surface as he thought back to his ex-wife's fight with cancer. He tuned into Mattie to keep his mind in the present moment.

"She's doing a lot better." Mattie said as a matter of fact as the strapped their seatbelts on.

Kendal paid the garage attendant as they exited.

"I know you're famished honey, anything in particular?" He asked pulling out into light traffic.

Several restaurants frequented the hospital area. In fact, with Ohio State nearby, this area had become a national test market for food eateries. As they passed a strip mall with different restaurants in it, Mattie was drawn to an old burger place that she and Cindy had loved as teenagers.

Being on edge with nervous energy for the past five days had a strange effect on Mattie's appetite. She hadn't had any desire to eat anything. Sheila and Geri forced her to eat, but half-sandwiches each day was not enough nourishment. Now, after being able to exhale slightly, she could feel the tension running up her back. A headache was pushing through her temples.

"Actually, yeah I can eat something. Can we stop at Johnny Rockets and grab a burger with some chili cheese fries?" Mattie asked, sounding enthusiastic for the first time in a while. She loved hamburgers with mayonnaise and American cheese, but she couldn't recall having a burger since she and Kendal had met.

"Did you know burgers were all I usually got when we went out?" Mattie added as he turned into the parking lot.

He had to slam on the brakes to his Audi A7 as a car leaving the strip mall failed to recognize incoming traffic and didn't stop.

Mattie reached over and blew his horn at the person driving the Chevrolet sedan, but she let her frustration subside by the time he pulled into the parking space.

"Thank you, baby for everything, all your support, and I am treating you for a change." Mattie paused as Kendal walked around the back of the SUV to open her door.

"I'm serious, don't reach for your wallet or credit cards." She stepped down from his trucks running boards putting her arm around his.

"And I'm ordering your food big daddy, in fact you're not allowed to speak or even look at our server. I'm in charge." Mattie leaned into him as they walked into the burger and shake shop.

"Is that right?"

"Uhm yeah, that's right, all eyes on me." She said nudging him back.

"Ok Tupac, I guess you are in charge, I can't even look at our server?" He smiled opening the door to the restaurant.

After being seated, Mattie reiterated that Kendal wasn't supposed to say a word. She ordered strawberry lemonade for him and a Sprite for herself, since they didn't serve Pepsi products.

The waiter didn't understand what was going on when he returned with the drinks and asked what they wanted to order.

"Big Daddy is going to have a chicken sandwich with onion rings, and I'll have a single with mayonnaise and cheese only, plus chili cheese fries."

The waiter chuckled when she said, 'Big Daddy'.

"Is that my new nickname?" Kendal asked, but she cut him off.

"I haven't decided what your nickname is going to be Kendal Abraham." She replied laughing out loud, so loud that the other patrons looked towards their booth. For the first time in days Mattie felt alive again.

As they ate, they talked about Grandma Redd's recovery and how long Aunt Penny was going to stay in town.

"She'll stay until the cows come home, she's the younger sister and the only one left out of nine kids. She's a stubborn woman and she loves family." She wanted to talk to Kendal about Grandma Redd giving her blessing, but she would wait until he was ready to bring it up.

"How do you feel about staying with me a couple of days next week?" Mattie asked him, as the waiter brought a refill of strawberry lemonade.

The waiter understood that Kendal was capable of speaking, but he still addressed Mattie directly adding to their dinner dynamic.

"Would you all like dessert or something else?" The red-haired server asked. He looked to be a college student, as did most of the servers on site.

"Big Daddy, you want something else to munch on." Mattie asked with a huge smile on her face knowing she had said it with all types of sexual innuendos.

The waiter's eyes got big and Kendal almost choked on his drink.

"Nope he's good, I gotta take him home for his special sweet treat, so you can just bring me the check." Mattie said winking at Kendal.

Her mood had been all over the place, but she was

beginning to find her center again to balance those same emotions.

"You might get the business if you're a good boy later." She said taking her foot to stroke his crotch under the table as people looked on. Kendal looked around the restaurant before replying.

"You keep rubbing on me right now and Johnny Rockets is gon be Johnny Rock that tail in a minute. Honey you gotta stop because I'm going to have to stand up in a second when we leave and I ain't trying to scare none of those kids." Kendal responded as she pushed his crotch one last time.

"Wasn't King Kong a good guy?" Mattie asked the waiter when he returned with the check.

"Uh, King Kong, yeah I guess, until they messed with his woman." He answered not fully comprehending.

Mattie's ring tone to her cell phone went off.

"Here take this and keep the change." She gave him a forty-percent tip before answering her phone.

"This is Mattie."

"Ms. Parks, this is Nurse Galloway, come now please...hurry I've got to go back." The nurses voice carried anxiousness.

Mattie heard the hospital intercom sound system calling 'code blue'.

"We're on the way." Mattie hung up the phone and snatched her purse off the table.

"We gotta go right now!" she was nervous as they ran out the restaurant back to the truck.

Kendal took shortcuts on the way back to the hospital staying off the main roads to avoid the lights. Kendal tossed his keys to the valet person walking out to his truck, before catching up to Mattie who was already running though the hospital door. She had scrambled through the first wing of the hospital and into the Intensive Care Unit.

Mattie saw nurses and two doctors walking out of Grandma Redd's room asking each other questions because they looked confused.

The corner of the glass pane hadn't been completely closed so Mattie saw the white sheet draped over the bed.

"No...no...no!" Mattie yelled loudly trying to get into the hospital room.

A male nurse tried to grab her to keep her out, but Kendal was back at her side and he forcefully pushed him into the nurse's station.

"Don't touch her!"

Nurse Galloway was walking out the room and her face was covered in disbelief.

"I need to see her." Mattie ignored one of the doctors tried speaking to her, as he attempted to tell Mattie to calm down.

"Don't fucking talk to me right now."

She didn't have time to hear anything from him or anyone right now; and she kept pushing through the mock defense.

"Madison, Ms. Parks come with me." Nurse Galloway ushered her into the room past everyone.

Doctor Prishnev was staring at the charts, going over them line by line and didn't notice who was entering the room as she spoke with herself.

"Everything looked better today than it did yesterday, I just don't understand it." Doctor Prishnev had no answers when Nurse Galloway walked Mattie to the head of the bed.

"Are you sure?" Nurse Galloway asked Mattie, before pulling the sheet back to reveal Grandma Redd's lifeless body.

Grandma Redd looked serene, like she knew that her time had come and perhaps that was the reason she asked Mattie to leave.

Mattie took a step closer and ran her fingers through her grandmothers' hair.

Kendal stood behind her with his hands at his side. This was Mattie's moment to say goodbye and he understood that. He was too stunned, trying to comprehend what could have possibly happened in the short period of time that they had left.

"Ms. Parks we are sorry…her vitals," the doctor attempted to say, but Mattie held her hand up asking for a moment to say goodbye before listening to the cause of death.

Mattie looked down at her grandmother's face, her nose and eyes…her cheekbones. Mattie had a lot of her Native American features. Mattie's ideas on life and death, love and family had been shaped by this woman. She thought about the support and guidance she had been given, all the lessons on matters of the heart and spirit provided by her grandmother. She was the only connection she had with her mother finishing a prison sentence.

Mattie felt her body getting hot, she couldn't breathe. Her attempt to push through her light headedness was futile.

"I'm, I'm…I'm kinda hot." Mattie wobbled and passed out with Kendal barely catching her before she hit her head on the floor.

Chapter 6

THICKER THAN MOLASSES

When her eyes opened, Mattie was staring up at the ceiling as if she was looking at something.

She was lying on her back in a hospital bed being monitored. Kendal stood next to the bed and her two friends were sitting on the opposite side of the bed in chairs.

Mattie attempted to regain her focus but found that she

needed to be patient. She was fathoming if the conversation she just had with her grandmother was only a dream when it felt very real.

"It's my time baby, be strong and faithful." Were the last words Mattie remembered hearing before waking up.

"Baby." Kendal assisted as she tried sitting up.

"No, lay back." His eyes were red, but he kept his emotions to himself the best he could because Mattie needed his strength.

Geri and Cindy were dressed in sweatpants and sneakers. Cindy wore a red bandana wrapped around her head and had an unreadable expression.

"I...I just talked with grandma." Mattie said knowing those five words were extraordinary in this moment, but she didn't care.

Geri and Cindy glanced at each other before looking at Mattie lying in the bed and it was followed with an awkward silence.

"I'm ok, really. I'm ok. We have to make phone calls and arrangements, so I'm going to need everyone to help."

Mattie took her time to sit up.

"Baby, hand me my tennis shoes please." She swung her legs over the side, without any agitation in her voice.

Kendal slipped them on her feet with a puzzled look on his face.

Geri and Cindy stood up moving slowly, they would bear the brunt of the emotional outpour because the loss would affect her on a much deeper level.

"Please you two, cut that out." Mattie walked over to where they were positioned to hug them.

"We're family, thicker than molasses." Mattie held on to them both, repeating what Sheila had conveyed earlier.

Cindy started to cry, but Mattie told her 'everything will be ok'.

Nurse Galloway came in and looked at the chart at the base of the bed. She advised Mattie to sit back down so she could check her blood pressure and pulse. After handing Mattie two pills to take and a glass of water, the nurse gave Kendal a prescription that Dr. Phrishnev had written for Mattie.

"Get these filled for her and we will have the test results back in a few days, but she needs as much rest as possible and Ms. Parks, I am so, so sorry for your loss."

Nurse Galloway was genuinely sympathetic; and felt akin to Mattie's close-knit family.

"Thank you, you made a real difference and I won't, no…we won't forget all the care, but we have arrangements to make for her. We can call you for anything if we have questions?" Mattie touched the nurse on her hand.

"Of course, call or just have Sheila get a hold of me. I won't intrude anymore." Nurse Galloway excused herself, removing the clipboard from the bed before exiting the room.

"We're going to go to Kendal's tonight; I've got to get grandma's belongings first." Mattie tried to say but Cindy spoke up.

"I'll get, we'll get it Mattie and take it to your house." She said wiping her eyes again.

"Yeah we can do that." Geri followed Cindy's lead, they were hoping Kendal was on their same page, but they couldn't be sure until he spoke.

"Your sisters can handle that baby; the doctor said you needed to rest. You can make any calls from the house, but let's get out of here. It's been a long day and we have a lot of arrangements, anything else we need here?" Kendal asked picking Mattie's purse up from the corner of the hospital bed.

"Ok." Was all she responded with; she knew he was right about leaving.

Mattie saw how her friends were looking at her.

"I'm ok, more than you know, seriously."

People were gathered around the nurse's station. Nurse Galloway was typing something onto the computer and the male nurse Kendal had pushed was standing up from the desk.

"Hold on honey." Kendal let Mattie's hand go as he walked over to the station.

"Hey brother, I meant no offense earlier." Kendal said putting both of his hands on the counter.

The male nurse had been upset when it happened, but after realizing they just lost a family member, the nurse calmed down.

"No, it's ok, I probably shouldn't have tried to intervene, I was out of place. I'm truly sorry about your loss." He reached out to shake Kendal's hand and offered more condolences.

Mattie saw people walking into the hospital supporting a pregnant woman while someone rushed past them in a wheelchair; the woman was in labor.

"The circle of life requires us to take care of those we love," Mattie thought reliving the conversation she believed she had when she was passed out.

"It was real." she mumbled.

"You want me to stop by the pharmacy first or you want to just get home?" Kendal pulled out of the hospital garage for a second time in the same night.

"No tomorrow is fine. I'll need to be on the phone for a while tonight. When we get home can you look up funeral services for me?" Mattie asked feeling empty inside. It wasn't complete sorrow as she stared out the window watching the streetlights fade in and out against the dark background.

She was searching her recent memories of the conversation she had with her grandmother so she could write it down, for now, she was putting them into the note application on her cell phone.

"I've lived a full life and I'm going home." It was more flashes of pictures than actual words she was remembering. Mattie stared out the window of the truck seeing her reflection in the Audi A7's mirror. She saw her face, but something was different beneath it she just couldn't put her finger on it.

"I can handle that baby." Kendal's voice broke through answering her question. He wasn't as talkative as usual, but Mattie could feel his support even in his silence.

The drive seemed longer than usual and after arriving back at his condo he made tea with lemon and honey.

Mattie sat at his dining room table with a yellow legal pad, writing down what had to be done for the funeral. Kendal made phone calls, having to leave some messages to get rates and comparison of what their services entailed.

He wrote three different names on a separate pad and slid it next to her to look at when she had time. He placed an asterisk that the church and Pastor Morris could provide the service, something he figured Mattie overlooked with so much on her mind.

Mattie made over fifteen phone calls after speaking with Pastor Morris who called her cell phone to offer his condolences and services for the family. The funeral would be held on the following Thursday giving family and friends time to travel from the south and east coast." Mattie took a shower with Kendal and then they prayed together before falling asleep.

CHAPTER 7

THE DAY AFTER

Mattic was up at five thirty in the morning putting on sweats and sneakers. She was pulling her sweatshirt over her head when Kendal turned over.

"Baby, you ok?" he asked propping his head up on the pillow.

"I'm good, just wanna run this morning, go back to sleep." She replied bending down to tie her shoelaces.

"You want me to go with you?" He asked still half sleep and naked.

"No, I'm gonna to run and clear my head; I couldn't sleep, just get some rest." She gave him a peck on his lips before walking down the stairs from his loft area and out the front door.

The morning air hit her first, it was a heavy breeze and the sky was overcast. She stretched, did fifty pushups and one hundred crunches, before doing twenty-five jumping jacks to loosen her limbs. She opened a music application on her iPhone to listen to music through her air pods during this quick exercise.

Kendal's condo community was about two miles in diameter. Land not developed yet; it would be under construction soon.

The large man-made pond and runoffs were the central point of the area. The other acres were being prepped for new homes and as Mattie ran, she saw people pulling out of driveways with their headlights on. Some waved at her through their car windows to acknowledge her. Mattie nodded back at them, throwing her hand up in response and kept running.

This housing development was gated with three separate entrances into it. It was set up as one huge oval and spread throughout with various trees and shrubs separating the homes already occupied.

The landscaping was impeccable, multicolored plants were everywhere and the bushes cut and manicured. Each lawn was cut to resemble the same pattern, regardless of the design selected as the home.

As Mattie ran, she fell deep into her memories. She thought about her grandmother sitting in her chair crocheting; the times she sat in the stands at her track meets or martial arts tournaments during high school and college.

Each step she ran took her back to the moments in her life where the paths crossed; she always had been influenced by her grandmother. Now she had to influence herself, now she had to live without her foundation.

Mattie hadn't paid attention to her pace, she ran hard.

She imagined the people responsible for the whole ordeal and got upset knowing that the police didn't have any leads. Henry wasn't assigned to the case, but he monitored it daily, as he moved up in the ranks, doing what he had intended when he first joined the police force.

Mattie imagined the intruders hitting her grandmother and pushing her into the wooden hutch and she ran faster. She thought back to all the tubes going down her grandmother's throat and pushed herself harder around the pond.

Kendal's place was in sight, so she throttled down.

Her breathing was sporadic, and she knew she had run the circumference of the neighborhood fast, faster than she intended. She felt like she had to spit, but her mouth was dry. She had not taken water with her.

Mattie was only about two hundred yards from his front door, and she knew better than to sit down so she tried to stretch her hamstrings, but they were beginning to cramp. She managed by walking slowly down the road. Her calf muscles tightened as she stepped through the front door. She dragged herself into the kitchen, grabbed two bottled waters and then fell out in the middle of the living room floor.

Kendal was up already taking a shower. Mattie smelled

the coffee being made but she was still cramping, or she would have made his cup for him.

"Damn baby you just run a half-marathon?" He asked stepping out the door of his lower level bathroom with a dark blue towel wrapped around his waist. His gold chain and Nefertiti bust laid in between his chest cavity.

Mattie held her arm for him to lift her.

"I ran too hard, just give me a sec." She gingerly walked to sit down at the dining room table.

"You want a cup of coffee, might give you a little jolt?" Kendal asked walking into the kitchen.

"No, no honey," Mattie paused to take a big gulp from a water bottle.

"Pepsi in a glass with ice please." She finished.

Kendal opened the two liter of Pepsi and poured, he took a sip and a frown appeared on his face.

"Ooh wee, I'll stick to my morning kick." He kissed her on the lips before handing her the glass.

"Do you want me to meet with you and Pastor Morris

later?"

Kendal sat down at the table, opposite of Mattie. Pastor Morris wanted to speak with her in person about the arrangements, but he also wanted to counsel her.

"No, I'll go and take Sheila with me; will you pick out stationary cards and a guestbook?" Mattie answered him and then drank the rest of the bottled water before downing the Pepsi.

"Yeah, I got that covered. You know I haven't said much, I am so sorry." he started to say but she cut him off.

"It's ok, thank you honey."

She hesitated again.

"When I passed out, she spoke to me." Mattie peered down into her Pepsi glass, slowly raising her eyes to stare at him.

"Is that right?" Kendal didn't want to show any surprise at being told about her vision.

"She told me she was going home, to stay committed and faithful. I remember her saying who I am will hold me together and then I was staring at the ceiling in the hospital room." She finished taking another drink of soda.

Kendal took a sip of coffee from a University of Tennessee mug.

"There are many accounts of family and loved ones being contacted after their member has passed away. I used to have very vivid dreams after Janine passed, but nothing as personal as what you witnessed. It took me a year of therapy to move forward. This is just the beginning baby. You should write down what you remember, put to paper your emotions as an outlet to those things you can't fully share with anyone yet." Kendal took another sip of coffee.

"That's a good idea honey, I think I will…" she hesitated again as she looked at Kendal, thinking about how he had never left her side since the first day of the tragedy. She recognized that his obligation to the center was important, but he stayed with her.

The paperboy throwing the daily newspaper onto Kendal's entry caught their attention. He rode a bike with his bag strapped over his shoulder so he could reach into it and toss a paper with more efficiency. Mattie had no idea why the paperboy fascinated her.

"I love you Kendal Abraham Scott, have you decided about the tour?" she asked completely changing the topic.

Mattie knew how important it was to him and how he prepared for it, that same night her grandmother was sent to the hospital. Kwame had called him several times to check on the condition of Ms. Redd, but both times he asked Kendal about his decision. Kwame had put his reputation on the line, something Kendal hadn't forgotten, so Kendal promised him by Friday, the original deadline, he would have his answer and his friend completely understood.

"No, I haven't. I was going to worry about it after we took care of everything, there will be other tours baby." He said standing from the table to go get dressed. He kissed her on the cheek before walking upstairs to the upper loft area. Mattie sat at the table and drank down the rest of her Pepsi. She looked down at the legal pad and checked a few items off the list. She knew at the time of the service she would be emotional, but for right now she was going to make sure Grandma Redd's memorial was the perfect 'going home' present that could be given.

CHAPTER 8

A PENNY FOR A THOUGHT

Pastor Morris gave the perfect memorial service for Grandma Redd. He spoke of all the positive attributes that she had possessed. Faithfulness and servitude, loyalty, and a commitment to family; he used Mattie as an example to what Grandma Redd had accomplished.

"Have no worry, Amadahy Redd is in Heaven with the angels and saints" he said.

Not too many people knew her first name was a Cherokee name meaning 'forest water'.

The church was overcrowded with people paying their respects to Mattie's grandmother, a lot of people she had never seen before. Some were Grandma Redd's old students. She had taught and tutored high school mathematics multiple years. The former students were all older than Mattie, but they had come to share a final goodbye.

Aunt Penny sat next to Mattie, and Kendal sat on the other side of her. Other family members were spread out in the first pew, along with Geri and Cindy who sat at the end of the row. Sheila and her kids sat in the pew behind them along with David and Camille, because of space.

Kendal, Henry and David were pall bearers, along with Sheila's two brothers and two deacons from the church.

Mattie felt sorrow and loss, but not the depth of emotional pain that Aunt Penny was feeling as she cried and yelled. Mattie had tears rolling down her face as they covered the casket with dirt. She, along with a few members of the family, stayed behind to make sure she had been properly secured.

Aunt Penny was still petitioning to have her sister buried on the family property in Georgia, but she was willing to table her opinion until later.

Aunt Penny let out a loud scream as the last bit of dirt had been put on top of the grave site. Kendal supported Aunt Penny to the limousine, leaving Mattie to walk with Cindy and Geri who were consoling her.

Boxes of tissues had been exhausted, and many more were being opened in the back of the long black car, and the ride back to the church was intolerably silent. Mattie didn't want to go back, but she had to serve food to those guests deciding to stay.

As people ate in the dining area of the sanctuary, Mattie spoke with people, a lot of them she didn't know or couldn't remember from the years passed.

The first two hours weren't so bad, but she didn't know how many more "I haven't seen you since or; wow you sure have grown up" she could take.

Mattie would not have found the patience if this had not been for her grandmother's celebration of life.

Kendal was a rock for Mattie. His strength and

attentiveness to her needs lessened her burden. He made sure that if she was getting frustrated, he interjected into the conversation to shift the focus from her.

Geri, Sheila and Cindy sat at the head table with them. Some people's faces showed that they didn't understand what part of the family 'the white girl' was on, but they remained cordial and respectful after Mattie introduced all three of them as her sisters. David and Camille sitting at the family table was also a topic of conversation.

"Cynthia, she would have enjoyed that very much." Sheila mentioned the song Cindy had chosen to sing for the memorial service. Her voice filled the sanctuary, stirring every soul and spirit in attendance.

Cindy had tears flowing down her face from the very first note to the final amen, but everyone, including the older people, had stood halfway through her rendition of "God Has Smiled on Me", Grandma Redd's favorite song. A few members of the church choir walked on stage with her as she sang to accompany her.

"Yeah, I was already a wreck but that took me over. You know she wanted you both to sing in the choir, she would've loved it." Geri added moving her food around with her fork but like the others, she didn't have an appetite.

Kendal had everything catered from his old restaurants and had his parents bring it down in one of their vans. He still owned a percent of the restaurants, plus he still held the patent for the barbecue sauce.

His parents didn't stay to eat. They left after the internment because Doug Sr. had an appointment to check the function of his kidney that couldn't be rescheduled for another three months. He would've put the appointment off, but Kendal and Mattie begged him to go get checked.

Mattie had overlooked calling her Colombian family until the day before the going home services. She simply forgot being so overwhelmed, but Sheila had phoned David. David and his fiancé flew out from Seattle, to support Mattie. Senora Rojas understood, but promised Mattie she would be visiting Ohio to care for her. Mattie welcomed her arrival.

"I'll have to take this with me, it smells good, looks good, but I ain't got no appetite." Cindy whispered to Geri as an older couple walked towards the head table.

"Young woman you have a beautiful voice, an angels voice." The woman extended her hand to Cindy and then to her other two friends. She had a red undertone in her complexion and dark black hair.

"Thank you, ma'am." Cindy responded with a smile being polite. Geri and Sheila were shaking hands as people came to give them a final goodbye before leaving the memorial, returning to their cities and home states.

"Thank you all so much for coming, she would be grateful to know that so many people came, she always believed in service and now we all see the fruits of her labor by those who cherished her." Mattie spoke with the older couple who were now hugging Aunt Penny, they looked vaguely familiar.

Mattie noticed people; women from the church group and deacons cleaning up the tables that were no longer being used.

"Madison, you make sure if you need anything you can call us, we cousins." The older man said. He was still holding onto the itinerary from the memorial service.

Mattie's height, he was bald on the top of his head with little strands of gray hair on the side.

Aunt Penny favored Grandma Redd, but she was thin, and light-skinned like Mattie. Mattie favored her temperament more than she did her grandmothers.

Grandma Redd would tell Mattie 'you get too emotional, you act like your Aunt Penny, but she just flat out hot headed from start to finish.'

"Madison, this is your cousin Ed and Lorene from Tennessee." Aunt Penny said seeing Mattie look awkwardly at them.

"Galilahi, don't worry about that, she ain't seen us since she was like eleven years old, but we gon do much better than that from now on." Lorene adjusted her glasses from slipping down her nose. She had a light gray dress on with a matching woman's hat, while Ed wore an eggshell colored suit with a green shirt and green tie.

"Galili...who?" Mattie said not knowing where that name came from. She knew her grandmother had a Cherokee name but didn't think too much beyond that.

"Galilahi child, that's my Cherokee name, it means

'attractive', your grandmother didn't tell you that? Her name means forest water, but enough of that, do you remember yo kinfolk?" Aunt Penny asked motioning back to them.

"I kinda remember y'all, it's just been so long, thank you for all the family support." Mattie finished by hugging Lorene and shaking Ed's hand.

Aunt Penny carried on a conversation with them while Mattie said goodbye to other people, filtering some of the ones she didn't know towards her friends.

Kendal was talking to Pastor Morris shaking his hand. Mattie thought he was thanking him for everything, but couldn't be sure because the pastor was holding his Bible and something else in his hand. It looked like a small black notepad. Kendal handed Pastor Morris an ink pen to write something into it and then gave Kendal a fist bump.

"Lala, are you going back to the kitchen?" Geri stepped away from the table moving through groups of people congregating.

"Yeah they're going to wrap this up, and I'm sure Darian and Sam are gonna want more to eat later when they go back to their dads place." Sheila answered watching her kids sit at the table with their father James.

"Please put some stuff in there for Cindy and me, we'll get it later, I have to smoke something. I haven't had an appetite all damn week.

"Yeah I'm gonna take a box of stuff, I don't think I've had anything to eat in two days either, so have them make something up for me too." Sheila and Geri walked over to her kids table.

"You guys doing ok?" Sheila asked her children who were scribbling with crayons on the table napkins, but James responded first.

"Hey, I've got to get going, you want to have them sit them up there with y'all?" he asked.

He didn't look Sheila in the face when he said it.

Sheila looked at Geri and just shook her head back and forth.

"I'll take em Lala." Geri waved her parents down before they left to catch a plane back to Wisconsin. Her mother owned a small clothing store with high priced goods she purchased after leaving her law practice, and her father, also an attorney, was ready to retire.

"Come on little munchkins, y'all can come say goodbye to my parents." Geri rubbed the top of their heads before leading them away.

"Thanks Geraldine." James spoke out but Geri ignored him while walking away with the children.

"I thought you were taking them today." Sheila did not fully understand why the plan was changing.

"Yeah, I know I was, but something came up at the last minute that I have to address, my weekend doesn't technically start till tomorrow so what are you tripping about Sheila?"

"You know what don't even worry about it. I don't have time to even have this conversation with you right now because it's just not appropriate." She held a large amount of displeasure in her voice; she didn't yell but the disappointment came through loud and clear.

"What's that mean, I help provide for them." James tried saying but Sheila followed Geri's path and walked away from him.

Cindy saw what was happening and tried to pull away from a group of people offering condolences and complimenting her on the song, but she couldn't stop the dialogue in time.

James grabbed his coat from the back of his chair and walked out the lower level of the sanctuary without saying goodbye to anyone, including his children.

Sheila followed behind Geri saying goodbye to her parents who had made the trip from Whitefish, Wisconsin. She then excused herself, walked into the kitchen and began loading a few boxes of food and helping clean the kitchen area. She could be productive and left alone for a moment.

Geri pushed the double doors open to the kitchen and walked over to where Sheila was standing. She grabbed a kitchen towel and cleaning bottle and began wiping down the stainless-steel tabletops.

"His weekend don't start till tomorrow, that's what that muthafucka said, why did I have kids with him, why did I even marry his sorry ass!" Sheila paused to lower her voice.

"He wants to play that shit, I'll be like him from now on and take his raggedy ass back to court, do you know he just signed a contract to supply all the labor for the buildings for the downtown renovation, he don't know I know, but if he wants to play like a fucking clown, I'll put the wig and red nose on his ass." Sheila ended the conversation as First Lady Morris walked into the kitchen.

"Madison is so blessed today, I've never known a group of friends as close as you all, I haven't known that many women who share the type of sisterhood you four ladies do."

First Lady Morris didn't hesitate to add elbow grease to the cleaning.

"God is so good to us; Grandma Redd was so proud of all of you." She followed up before giving details to other people helping in the cleanup process.

Sheila wanted to help Mattie finish out the day so she had already asked James to take the kids one day early, but she would never ask him for anything again, except for what the divorce and child support agreement contained. So, as she walked out of the kitchen and back into the dining area, she let all the bullshit slide away because most of the important people that really mattered were standing around the main table.

"Mommy, can we go to Auntie G's?" Samantha asked as Sheila approached with Geri right behind her.

"I figured I could take them with me since you all are going to be here a little longer." Geri understood that Sheila and Cindy would remain until the very end. Geri had planned on staying, but with James leaving the kids behind, she believed it easier to take them away.

"Yeah that's a good idea and I'll call you when we're leaving." Sheila answered

"You both hung in there like the big kids, y'all did really good." Mattie spoke out to Darian and Samantha as she approached, leaving Cindy to tend for herself with people wanting her to sing at weddings and other events.

Cindy declined each invitation; her singing days were over.

"I miss grandma." Samantha said looking sad like everyone else.

She wanted to be more mature, but she couldn't help

crying throughout the day. Mattie was curious as to how a child could experience the same anguish; her conclusion was all things were relative and with that revelation, Samantha had a right to be saddened.

"Well we will miss her together, but as long as we remember her, she will always be with us." Mattie reached down and wrapped her arms around the pre-adolescent girl. She didn't know who needed it more between the two, but she held onto Samantha a little longer than expected.

Cindy appeared and pushed in between Sheila and Geri. She scanned over her shoulder slowly so she wouldn't be obvious.

"I don't mind speaking to idiots, but peons are another story. If you're going to dip and leave, give me a heads up. I'm over there talking to Ed, Fred and Barney. I hope cousin Lorene knows her husband plans on leaving her once he takes care of his money situation." Cindy returned her attention back to the group.

"Oh, and Aunt Penny is ready to go, she's tired and worn out and she told me to tell you that." Cindy finished with a fake smile directed at someone waving goodbye to them.

"I can take her to your house Mattie if you want, when the kids and I leave." Geri looked over at the table, Mattie's aunt was still sitting down drinking her fruit punch from a Styrofoam cup and waving a paper fan back and forth to cool her body off.

She was wearing all white, but it had gotten hot in the large room. Nearly everyone wore white because Grandma Redd had made it clear that her Celebration of Life was to be a joyous occasion and only the pastor could where black. She made them all promise years ago to wear white and Cynthia was to sing at her memorial, a song of her choice which is why when she sang, the tears flowed, but she still maintained control of her voice.

"She's feisty Geri, real feisty." Mattie wanted to prepare her friend for anything that might happen on the drive home with her aunt. Aunt Penny hadn't been very social since arriving from Georgia a few days prior.

"I got everything under control, your alarm code still the same?" Geri asked as Sheila hugged her children goodbye and told them to be on their best behavior or Auntie G had permission to discipline them.

"Yeah, it's the same and don't set it when you leave. I

don't want her opening a door and having the police show up." Mattie hoped her aunt would decide to leave in a day or two.

"Well, tell her I'm going to be taking her. Do you all have anything to bring to my house?' Geri focused back on the kids.

"No, ma'am, and Auntie G, can we play the video game at your house?" Darian knew that she had a new PlayStation 4 console unopened with two video games. Geri bought it for Darian, but Sheila asked Geri to keep it at her house since he had one bad grade in school.

"Are your grades better? Your mom didn't want you playing with it because your grades weren't good. Are his grades better Lala?"

Sheila's eyes lightened as she responded.

"Yup…way better." Sheila put arm on her son's shoulder.

"Then yeah y'all can play just take care of it, don't throw it around because you're a poor sport like your Auntie Mattie."

Mattie played video games years ago with her ex-boyfriend Brian, but she broke his console after catching him cheating, by throwing it out the window of his apartment.

Mattie walked away as they talked; she had to get her aunt back to Georgia as soon as possible so she could mourn in her own way.

Mattie stood by her aunt and said her last goodbyes to older family members and their children who had driven up from Tennessee, Georgia and other states.

Geri and Mattie made eye contact that it was time to go, so Mattie interrupted the family members speaking with Aunt Penny.

"Are you rushing me Madison? I did say I was ready to go so that's alright, yeah that's alright." Aunt Penny walked away without waiting for a reply from her niece.

Mattie pursed her lips, because she didn't know what to say to her elder having a conversation with herself. She followed behind her aunt, carrying the itinerary of the memorial service in her hand.

"Ready young lady?" She approached Geri with Sheila's children at her side.

"Absolutely Auntie." Geri affirmed taking hold of both Darian and Samantha to lead the way out of the dining area.

Mattie didn't know how she would have survived this far had God not put these people in her life.

Kendal had been helping the cleanup crew, who consisted of varied church personnel along with Deacon Terence Ector, who found the humility to apologize for the uncalled conversation when Terence spoke out of turn about Kendal's spiritual walk.

"Baby, we're almost done. I've got the guest book and pictures in the back of the truck already. I can help Pastor Morris and the deacons if you're ready to go. I'll come over if you decide to stay at your place." Kendal wiped a bit of sweat from his forehead with a leftover napkin from the ceremony. His sleeves, both rolled up, showed his tattoos, one on each forearm.

"Can you just stay with me?"

She rested her head on his chest.

He kissed the top of her head and reached for her hand.

"Of course, will your aunt mind, you said she's strict and

I don't want to be getting fussed at or cussed out. Everybody is dealing with emotions the best way they know how?" It was a simple sign of respecting her as an elder, although Grandma Redd had approved, there were too many unbalanced feelings to assume.

"Come over, it's my house and I'm grown." Mattie took a deep breath and looked around.

Everyone had departed besides the church members volunteering their time. Two deacons were mopping the floors pushing yellow buckets with soapy water in them, and First Lady Morris was waving at someone in their party to get their attention. She hurried down the three small steps of the stage and motioned towards the kitchen.

"We loaded three boxes of food to hold you over, I'm going to be checking on you for a while Sister Parks, and if I leave a message, I expect a phone call within forty-eight hours." She hugged Mattie.

"Kendal, Pastor wants a word with you before you head out." She finished as Cindy and Sheila were walking back from the kitchen being followed by other women of the church. A small silver cart on wheels followed behind them towards the exit with aluminum containers and multiple paper bags filled with food.

"We're gonna situate this stuff." Cindy explained moving along.

"How long you think you will be?" Mattie asked Kendal.

"I'm not sure, about twenty minutes to finish cleaning and who knows how long Pastor Morris will keep me. You have your key to the condo just in case you change your mind, if not I'll be there within the next couple of hours." He kissed her before she pulled away.

Kendal went the opposite direction to see what Pastor Morris required.

Mattie wondered what was going on between them; but burying her grandmother and making all the arrangements had taken the last bit of her energy and she couldn't think as clearly as she would like. She let the curiosity slip away and would just ask him later. Walking out of the church, Mattie began to think about all the events of the day, of the week; she felt lonely without her grandmother.

Sheila drove her minivan that day and Mattie said she wanted to lay down on the ride back. She pulled the middle seats forward to lay across the rear seat.

Cindy sat in the front.

Before Sheila had pulled completely out of the Church's parking lot, Mattie began crying uncontrollably. Cindy climbed in the back seat with Mattie and held onto her, joining in the tears, but silently.

BEREAVEMENT

Against the wishes of everybody, Mattie went back to work that following Monday morning. Her reasoning was that life moved on and so must she. She hadn't slept much waking up throughout the night the three days following the ceremony.

Aunt Penny hadn't decided when she was leaving. She advised Mattie that she would vacate the premises when she knew for a fact that her young niece was stable.

Grace, Kim and a few other people attended the memorial. Grace had helped with the flowers and made sure people signed the guest book.

"You don't look all that much better, why did you even bother coming in? You can take up to twelve weeks of paid time off." Grace had concern while watching Mattie forge through all the papers piled up on her desk.

She threw most of them away because nothing had really changed, nothing ever really changed at Global Entertainment.

"I know, but being home won't bring her back, plus Aunt Penny is starting to be all over my house. She found an old stash of *movies* that I hid in my office; in my closet and under a bunch of blankets. She told me she wasn't snooping around but they were all the way on the bottom, under all types of other stuff." Mattie laughed, plopping down into her cubicle's chair to spin around in a circle.

"These customers have not been so bad today. Just so you know Geno's head is on the chopping block, so he's been in here at least ten hours per day the last week."

Kim walked by with an oversized plastic cup filled with

ice water.

"Hey Mattie. Hey Ms. Grace." Kim moved to her desk. She sat down and logged into her computer system and started taking phone calls.

"That girl is ambitious as hell; she wants Geno's job." Grace paused to step closer to Mattie's desk with her long headset extension lengthening with her.

"You should take a little more time. The wound will heal eventually, you just need time, but if you're going to be stubborn as usual welcome back to the jungle." The older woman finished.

Mattie knew that Grace was coming from a place of love.

"Thank you for everything, Lord knows I would've been in a bad way had I been alone, so thank you if I haven't said it already." Mattie reached her hand towards the older woman and Grace reacted.

"Girl it's ok, hold on." Grace sat back down because a call was coming through her headset.

A few workers had signed a greeting card and left it on Mattie's desk.

'Grateful' was the word that came to her mind when she opened and read it. Mattie shook her head affirmatively as she put it up on her desk, the least she could do in acknowledgment of the card.

Mattie's computer was up and running so she reached into her filing cabinet for her headset. The cord was crinkled together so she untangled it, plugged in into the phone box so she could take a call.

"This is Madison, how may I help you?" she said adjusting her mouthpiece on the headset.

"Hi, Madison, what call center are you in?" A male's voice came through.

Normally Mattie would've simply said Ohio, but she was fumbling around with papers on her desk looking for an ink pen.

"Columbus," she replied.

There was an awkward silence between the two for a moment before Mattie asked for his account number to access it.

The man gave her the last four digits of his social security number. She wrote it down on a piece of paper, but it would be much easier, and less time spent on the phone if he had his account number.

"Thank you, sir, I actually need your account number to help you." She said politely scribbling on a scrap piece of paper to get the ink flowing from the pen.

"Eight two eight seven nine." There was agitation in his baritone voice.

"Thank you." Mattie replied courteously accessing his account, but she didn't know why he was breathing so heavily.

"Did you find my damn account Madison?" he asked changing the tone of the conversation.

Mattie felt her neck stiffening and tried to breathe easily. She didn't want any high-level escalated calls, especially on her very first one.

'Hard head makes a soft bottom.' she thought. She realized that she had come back too soon for the wrong reasons. Aunt Penny wasn't so bad, and maybe she needed Mattie to help her cope with losing the last of her siblings. After this call she would take more time off to grieve.

"Yes sir, I have the account up, may I have your name please?" She asked still being cordial.

"Don't you see my fuckin name on the account, are you stupid or something Madison in Columbus. My name is Jimmie Fredericks or J Fred."

Mattie could feel the aggression through her headset.

"Mr. Fredericks how can we help you today?" Mattie asked as the account notes were generating from previous inbound contacts from the customer.

"You can help me by answering one simple question, is there a woman named Grace that works there?"

Mattie didn't answer, instead she looked at the notes on the account and it was the same customer that had threatened Grace's life and cursed her over three months ago.

Anger wasn't the emotion Mattie was feeling now; it was much deeper than anger.

'Why are they letting him call back in here, he shouldn't even be allowed to keep his account' she thought.

Mattie gathered her wits, exhaled and sought to remain professional

"Mr. Fredericks I am not at liberty to discuss anything other than your account, is there something on your account you would like to address today?"

Mattie wasn't calling him sir anymore. He deserved another name that she wasn't allowed to say.

"Why do I get stupid bitches on the phone, bitch...bitch...beyotch! Well Madison in Columbus, since you want to act like that fuckin bitch Grace, I'm gonna come down there to your office so we can have this muthfuckin' conversation in person. I'll see what you can and can't answer in person, I bet you answer me then, Madison in Columbus."

Mattie tried getting control of the conversation,

"Mr. Fredericks if you have questions about your..."

"Did I tell you to speak? Did I say open yo mouth at all? You need to be disciplined too I see, so just shut the fuck up, because you can't even answer a question about a fucking old senile bitch that needs to be handled. She had the police showing up at my fucking house talking about I was holding someone hostage, thaaat slut wasn't no damn hostage, she can leave my property and be someone else's, but since she decided to stay I ain't got no hostages." he paused,

"Hey, bring yo stupid ass over here and apologize to them."

There was a moment of silence.

"Get yo ass over here muthafucka I ain't playing with you!" He yelled and Mattie could finally hear someone whimpering.

"Excuse me sir, you don't have to." Mattie tried speaking out, but he cut her off again.

"Shut the fuck up, shut the fuck up, shut theeeeee fuck up and accept the apology, that's all you gotta do."

"This trick don't know who the fuck I am. So tell her, tell this Madison in Columbus, who the fuck I am!"

Mattie wanted to go through the phone and beat him. She wanted to inflict as much damage as possible and teach him a lesson, but she couldn't, she was stuck listening to his sickness on the other end of her line.

"You're my everything." The woman gathered herself.

"Mr. Fredericks!" Mattie's voice intensified, but she stopped speaking when she heard the woman crying out.

"Please, I said it. Please no...no...no!"

Mattie thought back to how her father had abused her mother and tried taking her virginity. She imagined a man like Jimmie Fredericks being the one who broke into her home and killed her grandmother, her blood boiled.

"I told you Madison in Columbus don't open your gawd damn mouth, didn't I?" It sounded like he started man-handling the woman around his home.

Mattie was listening; emailing asset protection when she wanted to call the police directly, but that wasn't policy.

She figured, if she stayed on the line, the call was being recorded and it could deter him from seriously injuring the woman more than he had so far.

"Her name is Madison in Columbus, she's the stupid beyotch in my city that thinks she can talk to me any old way. Have you and Madison been conspiring against me? Is that why you been back talking me, when I tell you to shut the fuck up?

The sound of glass shattering echoed through the phone line.

"Your clumsy ass just broke my table. You see what you just made this tramp do Madison in Columbus? You're gonna pay for that table or your best friend Madison will!"

Grace looked over the cubicle, because she could hear his voice through Mattie's headset.

Mattie couldn't hear anything else coming from the woman.

"Wake the fuck up, you can thank Madison in Columbus." He hesitated and began threatening Mattie again.

"I'm going to come down there, to your job, since you can't connect me to Grace, and don't think I won't find out who you are Madison in Columbus. Tell your family their precious little girl is gonna have a visitor and there ain't shit those little security guards gon do to me." He went back to addressing the woman in his home.

"Get the fuck up, with yo dumb ass. See you soon

Madison in Columbus."

The line went dead.

Mattie was stunned. She stared at her computer screen as another phone call was coming through on her line. She hung up and logged out.

She ran out of her cubicle, almost knocking Geno over, heading to asset protection who had not returned her email.

A female asset officer was walking down the long corridor as Mattie rounded the corner.

"We got the email. I was just coming to get you. I'm sure we have enough evidence to forward to the police, but we have to get a statement from you too, can you, you think do it now?" She asked.

"Hell yeah, that man makes my blood boil, are the police on their way?" Mattie asked following the woman down the hall and through the locked door to the department.

The female asset officer had Mattie sit down at her desk without answering Mattie's question about what law enforcement was doing about it. Mattie noticed one of the pictures on the desk of her and a young male boy.

"Maureen, can you follow Rosalee, she's ghosting on FMLA."

A tall, white male coworker began to say not knowing Mattie was present.

"Oh, I'm sorry, come see me when you're done." He walked away.

"I'm sorry about that, let me write this part first and then write down your account of what happened." Maureen paused as she finished her portion by writing her id number on the paperwork.

"Ok, write down as much as you can recall, I'll be right back."

Mattie nodded and began writing; she was praying that the police saved the woman before any more damage could be done. Mattie had taken up two pieces of paper and Maureen had not returned yet. She sat for five additional minutes before leaving.

As she walked down the corridor, she wanted to know what he looked like.

Was he the type of man that hit her grandmother? Was he like her father when he used to abuse her mother?

She found herself back at her desk, sitting down staring at her computer screen.

'James Fredericks, 1416 Hillside Ave, Columbus, Ohio."

She stared at the information like it was a puzzle, trying to comprehend the thought pushing in her mind.

Slowly, Mattie took her ink pen and began writing down his name and address, followed with his social security number and date of birth. She took his cell phone number and credit cards listed on file.

She slid the piece of paper into her front jean pocket and sat there waiting another ten minutes for Maureen to follow up with her statement.

Mattie wrote a note to Grace and then turned her computer system off before handing the note to her older coworker. She whispered to her older coworker that she was leaving, taking her full 12 weeks of bereavement time.

'I got a call from the 'threatening' asshole, call me at lunch," the note read.

As Mattie's feet hit the pavement there was a loud crashing sound.

Two cars had just gotten into an accident on the opposite side of the street, with people behind them blowing their horns to tell them to move off to the side of the road instead of holding up traffic.

She sat down at one of the outdoor lunch tables waiting on her bus to come. She thought about going to the community center, but Kendal was on a conference call with investors for the Center's Program for at least another few hours.

Mattie took out the paper she had folded into her front pocket and read it all again. She found herself looking around for people watching her, she laughed for being so paranoid; and then chuckled again that she was laughing at herself.

"Stop being so damn silly."

She was still upset that James Fredericks treated people the way he did and upset at him for making her think about things in her distant and recent past.

"Did they pick him up?" Mattie kept wondering as she

waited.

Two buses stopped, letting people get off and on, but neither bus was hers. She had another ten minutes to sit.

'1416 Hillside' she thought wondering where it was. She felt the need to know, to know if he was in custody and what the coward looked like. She walked back into the building and bought a map of the city even though she could've googled it.

Sitting back, she studied the map looking for city markers to find the area of Hillside. The COTA driver blowing his horn at a car in the wrong lane passing the accident forced Mattie's eyes upward and her feet across the pavement to the bus stop.

She was going to find out the answers to some of her questions and by the time she had arrived home, a plan had formed.

She would pick a street near Hillside and program an address into her Global Positioning System. She would pack pepper spray, her butterfly knife, and her 9mm pistol in case something went sideways. She had no desire to engage in a physical altercation, but she wouldn't be a victim. Hillside was in an old rundown part of the city and she was not going to leave anything to chance.

Aunt Penny was in the kitchen frying up potatoes, peppers and sausage when Mattie walked in. It reminded her of her Grandmother, but Mattie didn't have an appetite for food, her curiosity was her hunger right now.

"You're back early; you want some of this concoction?"

Mattie shook her head no.

"I told you that you can't always stand in front of the bull, trust me child sometimes that bull get going and ain't nothing you can do about it."

Her aunt poured a glass of juice, made from a juicer that Mattie had not previously opened.

"Drink this if you ain't gon eat. I see it in yo eyes child. I feel the same thing you do Madison, but anger ain't useful right now; drink it all down." She finished turning back to stir the food on the stove, Aunt Penny was a lively spirit.

"Thank you, it's just more complicated gran…I mean auntie. I'm going to change and run some errands. My cell phone number is on the fridge and I'll set the alarm."

Mattie felt violated that Aunt Penny opened the juicer, even though it had been sitting in the box for over three months

"No, don't set that damn wireless Cuckoo Clock, hurting my damn ears. I'll lock all the doors and patio. If I step out and walk over to the park, I will set it, but not while I'm in here." Aunt Penny turned the burner off on the stove.

"If you leave, set the alarm auntie." Mattie reiterated, she was going to be very firm if her aunt said anything back in defiance, but she didn't.

Mattie drank down the juice and checked to make sure the patio door was locked. She went to her bedroom and changed her jeans and blue flip flops for an oversized jogging suit and tennis shoes. She threw the butterfly knife in her Velcro pocket and attached her pepper spray to her keys. She decided to wear a plain baseball cap to help cover her face. She checked her 9mm making sure it was loaded and slid it into her waistband holster.

"You want anything while I'm out? I'll be back in a little bit."

Aunt Penny was now sitting at the long couch with her

plate of food and juice, laughing out loud as she began watching an episode of Orange Is the New Black.

"No, I got everything I need honey," she paused as the television show went to commercial.

"Actually, where are the shells to the shotgun?" she pointed under the couch.

Mattie told her they were in the small utility closet, middle shelf in the box. She wondered where that question came from, because the shotgun was already loaded, but she wasn't going to waste time asking her aunt why she needed to know.

Mattie remembered that she left the piece of paper with the address to the customer in her jeans and ran back into her bedroom before leaving.

CHAPTER 10

1416

Traffic was minimal during the middle part of the day.

Fall had been in effect for months, but the constant fluctuation in temperature had today feeling more like late summer; pleasantly warm.

Certain trees and plants had lost their leaves and color, creating shades of orange, yellows and reds. Halloween decorations were in full effect, as the witches' holiday drew near.

Mattie didn't know what she would accomplish besides getting a visual of James Fredericks with her own two eyes. She wanted to know that the police were doing their job to ensure the woman's safety.

She input an address in her GPS for two city blocks away from Hillside and drove around until she ran across it.

A few kids rode their bikes, while other teenagers threw a football in the street after cars passed. They were taking advantage of their three-day weekend from school.

Mattie saw the house numbers were still declining as she moved forward. She found a parking spot between an old S10 pick-up truck and the corner.

Mattie pulled over and parked. She placed reflective sunglasses on and pulled her hat down across her forehead as low as it would travel.

A man wearing blue plaid golf shorts and a green t-shirt was mowing his grass on the opposite side of the street; when Mattie heard barking before she saw the dogs. Two pit bulls ran from behind a garage towards her, she didn't change her pace. Instead she ignored them as they were secured in a gated yard.

"Fuck 1416."

Mattie looked at the paper again. She had to walk two more blocks or turn around to go get her car and find another parking spot. She continued forward.

Mattie felt anxious as she got closer to 1416. A screen door flew open from a corner store, which made Mattie slow down to observe. Two young boys, one black and one white, came running out of the store with paper bags in their hands.

She heard boisterous laughter coming from inside the store, opposite from where she stood. This was an old neighborhood, once a middle-class haven of growth. It had faded into a minor resemblance of its greatness.

The two-story houses were built very close to each other and were elevated above the main road because of the way the land was structured.

She tugged on her hat out of nervousness, was she sweating because it was hot, she was uncertain. She ignored the small voice inside her head that kept telling her to turn around.

She finally arrived at 1416 Hillside.

There was an empty lot next to it with a large tree in between the driveway and the lot on the backside of the property. A thick silver chain was wrapped around the tree, and at the other end of the heavy linked chain was an older Rottweiler sitting down. Mattie couldn't determine the weight from the position while it rested its head on the ground. It watched as Mattie walked down the street towards the house but never moved.

A stray gray and black cat moving in the grass caught the dog's attention, and surprising the cat, it moved quicker than Mattie had imagined. The Rottweiler hopped up and began barking while pulling on the chain.

The explosive bass carried throughout the neighborhood and Mattie felt the vibrations in her body.

She didn't think anyone was in the house, due to no one checking to see what had agitated the large black and brown canine.

She slowed down, not knowing if she should turn around and walk back up the same side of the block. Instead she continued forward to the end of the street and crossed over before heading back up the opposite side.

She stopped at the same corner store the kids had run out of because she was thirsty. She was deep in thought as she took hold of the handle to the store's screen door.

"Why did I even come over here, what the hell was I going to do anyways?" More questions formed as she walked into the corner bodega.

A rack of chips and snacks ran down the middle of the store, splitting it in half. To the right of the chip rack, a small aisle was left open and opposite it was a counter to pay for merchandise. The counter had bootleg CD's and DVD's spread out under the glass case top nearest the register.

She walked down the row of coolers, shaking her head back and forth. Mattie had contempt that the beer and other alcoholic beverages she passed were prioritized before non-alcoholic beverages.

Her intent wasn't to listen to the conversation taking place between the worker and another man, but it carried throughout the small store.

"Dem lil ass kids was scared as hell dawg." The fair skinned employee sat behind the counter with a green cloth in his hand.

The other man was dark skinned and wore corn rows in his hair. He stood about six foot one inches, with a pot belly sticking out from his waistband.

Mattie thought it so passé that he had a cigarette fastened in between his ear.

"Hell yeah, they should be minding they own business, instead being all up in my shit asking why the po po is always at my spot. I shoulda whooped dey ass and then got some wet wet from dey fine ass momma later." The two men slapped hands while over exaggerating their laughter.

"You just raw dawg Jimmie, it's crazy how you and yo bruh's are so different. You get into trouble and they get yo ass outta trouble." The worker kept laughing.

"Fuck that, I git outta shit because my shit is ti-zight and I know how to spit game. I'm butta to beyotches fam, true pimp game homie." He finished looking back towards Mattie as she was pulled a Pepsi from one of the coolers.

Mattie still had her hat pulled down; through the beverage cooler she could see Jimmie looking at her in its' reflection.

Out of readiness she put her hand in her pocket and felt for her butterfly knife.

They started talking again, this time about The Deuce; a known neighborhood club that hosted many underground hip hop artists. This Halloween night after ten o'clock, it was half-off drinks and ladies could get in free.

"Yeah man, I'm gon be at dat muthafucka to see what the hoes talking, see if any of em qualified to be on my team." He grabbed his crotch trying to make eye contact with Mattie, but she hid behind her sunglasses.

As Mattie approached the counter, she had two single dollar bills in her hand. She tossed them onto the counter and lifted the Pepsi bottle up to show the store employee. She kept moving towards the door.

"I'm having tryouts for my squad little momma; a little Halloween party at The Deuce, swing by that joint and let J. Fred buy you a drank. You can wear a little outfit but no masks and shit, can't have nuckas trying to test they luck." His voice trailed off as Mattie walked out the screen door.

Her adrenaline was flowing because she hadn't planned

on being this close to him, she could smell the musk coming off his body. The butterfly knife had not left her hand since she made contact.

"You want yo change?" The worker screamed out, after opening the cash register.

"Naw dawg I'm straight." Mattie had not lost the hood authenticity in her voice.

"Two Saturday nights from now at The Deuce, beyotch." Jimmie yelled before the screen door closed behind.

Mattie could still hear them laughing at her.

She thought about how easy it would've been to cut one of Jimmie's major arteries with her knife, but that still would have left the employee and he hadn't threatened her. She had no idea if the store was being monitored on closed circuit and she was one hundred percent positive that there was a gun under the counter within the employee's reach.

Mattie walked quickly back up Hillside to her car. She hadn't opened her soda yet out of nerves. She got in, started her vehicle and turned right at the first street she was able.

"What the fuck was I thinking?" She asked herself while putting her gun into her console. She twisted the bottle cap off and took a sip.

"Always be prepared." The words flashed in her thoughts.

She then realized that there was a face to go with the name and he didn't suspect a thing. She also knew he had a brother, maybe an attorney or cop. More importantly, she knew in two weeks where to find him.

Mattie felt her mind racing again because she wasn't done with Jimmie. She had a little less than two weeks to plan something, and she knew she had to visit the bar to know its' layout.

Mattie drove around the block, but had trouble locating the bar initially. She did, however, approach two women working one of the world's oldest professions. She also recognized the signs of addiction. She waved them down after a few cars slowed to look at their product, but all passed on the product.

"What's happenin? Y'all know where Da Deuce is at?" Mattie asked adding the preposition at the end of the question purposefully.

"It's down there in da plaza, on the backside of da stores and shit, dem muthafucka's don't open up til around two tho boo." She wore a purple bra under a white fish netted top. Her ponytail was frazzled on the end. Mattie didn't judge because she knew the twists and turns that life could bring.

"Das wassup, gud lookin." She headed towards the plaza.

A grocery store and flea market took up most of the shopping area.

China King, an Asian restaurant, had neon lights flashing their daily special 'Four wings and fries for $5.25'.

Mattie made a U-turn and drove down what she originally thought was a street, but it turned out to be an alley behind the establishment. Instead of being in the front of the bar, she was in the back. She thought about making a U-turn, but she saw broken beer and wine bottles on the ground. She saw metal rods worn down from old fire escapes spread all over the pavement.

Mattie backed out slowly and drove around to the front.

Looking inside the front window from her vehicle, she got an image of the layout. Two pool tables and a dart board were opposite the bar area, but beyond that she would have to pay a visit when they opened. She looked at the hours of operation and read 3:00 pm-2:30 am.

The flyers and other advertising for the Halloween weekend bash was spread on the door and windows.

"Now what will I tell Kendal."

The thought was fleeting, she hadn't been one hundred percent in her commitment, but she was close. She knew she would have to take a closer look inside before the event if she chose to teach James Fredericks a lesson. The rest of her day she spent with her elder, going out to dinner and listening to her account of family history. Mattie had heard these same stories over the course of her life, but it was refreshing to hear her aunt's account expressing Grandma Redd's role in each story. Mattie laughed with her aunt and enjoyed an intimacy as they spoke about their departed loved one.

Chapter 11

BAIT

Henry had obvious concern on his face listening to one of the District Attorney's Paulette Shields tell them that Nickels' information contained some truth.

There had been hospital records of a woman fitting the description of Yvonne Fredericks admitted for facial trauma and bodily injury years ago, without her actual name as a patient on file.

"So, here's the tricky part, if he in fact has information

that can lead to the arrest and conviction of those involved in the triple homicide my office can work something out. Simply mentioning a name provides us nothing, but any corroboration of evidence that the family put the hit out we will provide him with protection." Paulette finished.

Her beige pant suit had small blue pinstripes in it that matched her blouse and the blue studded earrings that could be seen whenever her sandy brown curly hair was displaced as she talked.

Garrett didn't see the problem, he wanted to put Nickels back on the street as bait and watch who came to finish off the job of killing him.

His partner's appearance was disheveled, and Henry could smell the liquor from the previous night still permeating through his skin. He wasn't sure if his partner was being serious, but he knew that option wasn't feasible.

"How do we corroborate his story when the only other person present was killed during the shootout?" They understood that the death of his lifelong friend had been the catalyst to move the gangster to this point of cooperation.

"That's your job to figure out detectives. As you know,

moving against The

Fredericks is almost moving against The Mayor. My boss will do her job, but this has to be super tight or it's career suicide for all of us if we are wrong."

It was no secret the childhood bond shared between Mayor Blacksmith and Bob Fredericks; the man who had once been the subject of many criminal investigations. Now he had assumed a more legitimate business position, even helping segments of low-income families. His younger siblings, however, could not stay away from 'the life' and had not relinquished their grip on the drug business.

"We aren't trying to stir up the hornet's nest, but we have a job to do and wherever the leads take us is where we will go. The biggest question is…"

Henry was interrupted when the Captain barged into the meeting. He closed the door behind him and pulled the shade covering the glass.

"Counselor." He acknowledged Paulette.

"Officer Dansby; the officer on administrative leave, Kevin was found dead in his apartment. He hadn't reported in yesterday with his union representative and today, today that union rep found him dead from a single gunshot wound to the head."

The concern in his voice was apparent.

"That fucker killed himself." Garrett said, as more of a statement than a question causing Captain Turnkle to look his way.

"You look like shit." The Captain paused to let it sink in.

"And no, he didn't kill himself, it was made to look like that, but the bullet entered the right side of his head."

Paulette was unsure of the significance until Henry spoke up.

"He was left-handed." He said flatly.

"Who would want him dead, why kill him?" Paulette asked, wondering if the two cases were somehow intertwined.

Garrett adjusted his shirt and tie as he walked towards the window overlooking the parking lot. The picture he was forming in his mind was almost complete, but he couldn't see the entire connection between any of it yet.

Henry had a hunch and hoped he was wrong but as he began speaking, it gained traction.

"Kevin was pulled away from the patient's room for Arnold Poirten to kill a witness and murderer. The woman in charge that evening advised me that the nurse Kevin was speaking to was unfamiliar to her before entering the patient's room. What we know is this, Arnold has a partner, an on again off again lover who introduced him to murder for hire." Henry paused as it became even more clear.

"No hospital camera picked her up on its footage and no surveillance from the outside, meaning that."

The captain interjected again.

"She's cleaning up; eliminating anyone who could recognize her."

Paulette moved towards the round table and sat down. Although she had won a few major cases as an assistant district attorney, this was much more than what she expected on an early Monday morning.

"Partner did you get a good look at her face?" Garrett asked with concern in his voice.

Henry replayed the scene in his mind. His back was turned towards the room when Sheila noticed the patient's curtain drawn closed and she knew instantly that the nurse speaking with Kevin wasn't familiar.

"No, no I didn't but my friend, Sheila the nurse did. I need to call her." Henry said pulling his cell phone out.

"No, just wait, wait a minute." Captain Turnkle delayed Henry from making the call.

"No one can identify this woman, but what we do know is she will have information we can use against whoever hired her. This Sheila, we can put plain clothes on her at all times, it's probably the best shot we have,"

The captain was interrupted by Henry.

"To getting her killed. No, I'm not on board with that. She needs to know, and I am going to tell her. Write me up, fire me, but before I leave this room, she's getting a call from me." Henry added with fervor.

The silence that ensued was uncomfortable, but Paulette's raspy voice broke through the tension.

"Why can't we tell her and ask if she would be willing to

participate?" She asked as if it was too simple an equation to figure out.

"Captain?" Garrett asked waiting for an answer.

He knew Henry's mind was made up and what Paulette had offered was acceptable. He just didn't know how being threatened by Henry would move the captain's ego.

"Henry call her and see if we can get her in here ASAP. Find her location and I will assign as many plain clothes officers that I can, regardless of whether she agrees or not. There's no doubt that her life is in danger if the reports I've heard about this woman is true." Captain Turnkle added.

"What reports?" Paulette asked. Now that the cat was out of the bag, she needed to know more.

"Well they call her one of the best. She's killed on three different continents. If Kevin is truly one of her victim's, she now has over fifty confirmed kills and almost that many unconfirmed. She's versed in bomb making and clandestine tactics. Her last known whereabouts were that she resided in Las Vegas working for hire. She fled after killing an employer who tried double crossing her." He took a seat at the table with Paulette.

"How the fuck has all of this murder for hire made its way to our city. We are a great city, with a great college football team and a halfway decent hockey team. We don't get shootouts, and what else; oh yeah that's right international assassins for hire." Garrett approached Paulette.

"Nickels is the key right now, so we can offer him protection with viable information?" He asked pulling a chair out from the table to sit down.

"We can extend that offer, I will speak with his attorney and I think it would be a good idea to put him into protective custody immediately." Paulette had him detained for an outstanding warrant for failure to appear at court for a misdemeanor violation.

The three at the table continued to speak as Henry placed a call to Sheila, he left a voice message on both her cell phone and work voicemail to have her call him immediately. He had the Captain send officers to her job to secure her and bring her back, while he and Garrett assisted Paulette with Nickels and his attorney.

CHAPTER 12

EL FILETE

Sheila had gone to bed early the previous night after working the third double shift in as many days. She didn't necessarily enjoy the long hours, but she couldn't ask others to do what she was unwilling.

Samantha and Darian kissed her good morning and

goodbye, as she forced herself awake.

"Do you guys have everything? Your father won't have time to turn around and drive back?"

Sheila stretched her body while still in bed.

James was picking them up for one final trip to Hocking Hills, before their brief fall break was over. Sheila gave him permission to keep them out an additional day from school. He was taking them on a hike in Hocking Hills after settling into their cabin. Darian's birthday was in a few days, and he wanted to go to Old Man's Cave and ride horses.

"Mom, I packed everything on the list and double checked it after you fell asleep last night. I cleaned the dishes and kitchen stuff." Samantha was pulling her suitcase outside to her father's car after he blew the horn for a second time.

"Tell your father people are still sleeping at 6:30 in the morning and I have to be at work in a few hours."

"Mom it's 8:00."

Samantha yelled as she closed the front door behind

them.

Sheila panicked because her shift started in less than an hour.

She stumbled out of bed attempting to get her bearings and almost fell into her dresser. She had undressed last night and hopped into bed with her clothes and shoes in the middle of the room.

She showered quickly and put new scrubs on. She wrapped her micro braids into a ponytail and brushed her teeth, before walking into the kitchen to brew coffee. She smiled because the kitchen was spotless but as soon as she had a clear view of the living room, her joy turned sour.

Her children had been up late watching movies with snacks. Those snacks hadn't been cleaned. A bowl of popcorn was left on the coffee table. Empty energy drink aluminum cans were left on the floor. An empty container that once contained ice cream was sitting in the loveseat, and appeared to have melted into the fabric of the furniture.

Sheila didn't have time to clean any of it and vowed to leave it that way until her kids returned. It would also provide the reason they would face punishment, for not doing what they were asked, when they bartered to stay up late, along with an additional day from school.

Sheila grabbed her fresh brewed coffee and her keys from the key ring. She rushed out the back door, nearly stepping into the large puddle of water gathered in her rear entrance.

She had not fully awakened, and as she merged onto the highway the sounds of morning traffic filled the air. It wasn't until she parked in her designated spot, that she realized her purse and cell phone were left at home. Her second bout of frustration was kicking in.

The kids were with their dad and knew the number to the hospital for any emergency. She vowed that after this shift and overtime she would not see work again for at least two days.

When she walked into her office there were two notes about incidents on the patient's floor from the previous evening shift. It upset her that simple instructions weren't followed and now she had additional tasks for today.

She walked to the nurse's station and said good morning to coworkers. As if on cue, a patient was calling for assistance as the light to their room flashed.

"I got it." Sheila decided to jump head-first into today's challenges.

The patient had surgery recently and was experiencing pain as expected and didn't tolerate it well. Sheila knew that pain thresholds varied from patient to patient; and it wasn't that she didn't empathize with them, but she could not dispense medications before the required time, and this patient had been belligerent the day before.

"Good morning Mr. Harold." Sheila said fully expecting to hear complaints.

"What's so good? My fucking side is killing me and you're going to swear that I gotta wait for my pain meds, I already know. Well they were late giving them to me last night and I need them now!" He said staring at Sheila as he used the bed controls to lift himself up.

Sheila smiled and walked towards his equipment to check his vitals. His baldhead had grown stubble and his beard had grown over the last two days. The grey in his beard matched his chest hair sticking up from his gown.

Sheila caught herself before she laughed. She saw him as the old man emoji in her cell phone keyboard.

"Mr. Harold in fifty minutes I will come back and administer your medication personally. I understand your frustration last night at the staff but calling them derogatory names will not help your cause."

She knew he would challenge her as he did the first two days after surgery, but she had learned over the course of her career, be firm and kind.

"You will be back in fifty minutes? He asked with agitation in his voice

"Mr. Harold I will." Sheila affirmed.

"Ok, I can wait but that little queer nurse you have, I don't like him."

Sheila understood everyone wasn't acceptable of people in same sex relationships, but she knew the nurses under her care, regardless of sexual preferences, were extremely professional.

"Well Mr. Harold I will see you in fifty minutes." She excused herself without addressing the concern about the male nurse.

For the next forty-five minutes Sheila helped catch up on

charts, in between assisting a few doctors making their morning rounds. She returned to the nursing station to add patient information into the computer when she heard a familiar voice.

"I've called you three times, don't try and act like you been saving the world." Mattie exited the elevator, sliding her bookbag from her shoulders.

"I've been slammed since I got here, a sista was late on top of it all. James picked the kids up this morning. First chance I had after Grandma's service; I cussed his black ass out. When this shift is over, you're going with me for a couple of drinks." Sheila stood up from her desk to hug Mattie, before returning to finish putting the information on Mr. Harold's chart.

Mattie had no measurable reason to want to be at the hospital her grandmother had died in, but deep down she knew she was hoping for another sign.

The final conversation with her grandmother she accepted as true and this is what gave her the deepest comfort. She had learned to believe in other spiritual possibilities from spending time with her extended family, but more so from the private conversations shared with bisabuela in

Colombia.

She used visiting Sheila at work as an excuse, which in part was true, but there was more to it than that.

"Aunt Penny is being adamant about having Grandma's final resting place moved to Georgia along with her other siblings; am I wrong because I want her here with me, I mean am I being selfish?" Mattie paused before continuing, not allowing her friend to answer.

"You shoulda cussed his ass out, I know he can be "James", but he was one minute away from Kendal throwing him out of the reception." Mattie finished.

"I can't believe he showed his ass like that either. Something seemed off, like not normally off, but seriously off." Sheila sat back down at the nurse's station to finish the patient's chart.

The four small desks were used interchangeably by the staff of nurses in this unit. She was short staffed again, so she covered the additional shifts. Overtime paid her double time and a half so as she updated the records on the computer, she was earning nearly one hundred and twenty-five dollars per hour.

"Nope, don't do that. Don't give him excuses, he's a grown ass man and he could've definitely used his words better and showed more character all things considered."

Mattie leaned over the counter of the oval nurse's desk separating the hallway from their area. Her black calf-high boots lifted her up slightly, but Mattie had worn these for comfort knowing she would be on her feet most of the day visiting her friends at work.

Mattie had still not resumed any semblance of normalcy since the ceremony for her grandmother, but she wasn't as emotional. Partly because she had a support system of people who loved her. Largely because Grandma Redd had found her as she transitioned to let her know everything would be ok, and she was grateful Kendal understood.

Mattie had learned how to deal with Aunt Penny, the more she realized the loss her aunt felt burying her last sister. She knew her aunt needed support just as much as she did and with that, she found peace and patience attempting to build a deeper familial bond.

"Yeah, I know, you're right. I'm just saying over the past three months he has been, more, more, just better." Sheila paused because she realized she didn't need to continue making excuses for a man she divorced

"He was an ass." She finished, finally agreeing with her friend.

"On another note, I think Geri and Benelle are getting serious, well more serious than she wants to admit. She's stayed at his place twice in the past two weeks. She ain't fooling nobody."

Sheila stood from the desk to sign off on another chart.

"Yeah you're right, she ain't fooling nobody." Mattie repeated and shook her head in agreement.

A younger nurse approached twirling an ink pen between her fingers.

"I love your top, that's soooo disrespectful." She laughed uncontrollably with Mattie, when she walked into the nurse's station.

"Thank you, Sara believe it or not, that one over there got it for me," she nodded in Sheila's direction.

"Well I like her outfit too." Sara's scrubs were a match to Sheila's.

Sheila excused herself as she called out for Sara to accompany her, before she entered Mr. Harold's room.

"I'll be right back Mattie." Sheila disappeared into his room returning shortly to the nurse's station.

"I'm hungry, cafeteria for breakfast?" Sheila offered. Without hesitation Mattie obliged.

"Dammit I left my purse and phone." Sheila was exasperated.

"I got it, get drinks later."

The hospital cafeteria had tasteful foods. The area had expanded, and many of those employed selected this instead of other small food outlets surrounding the hospital.

"Hospital with a made-to-order omelet and waffle station but we can't get fully staffed. It blows my mind." Sheila took a sip of her orange juice. She had ordered biscuits and gravy and a side of asparagus.

Mattie had a full spread with waffles, an omelet with peppers and mushrooms, along with bacon. She enjoyed coffee with her meal and Sheila commented on Mattie dunking a portion of waffle into her coffee mug.

"Weird girl, just weird."

They both laughed.

Mattie ordered an espresso to go, with an extra shot. She was physically drained from her morning workout and needed a jolt of energy.

As they rode the elevator back, Mattie had an idea.

"I'll grab your stuff, but I'll have to use the Mystery Van, I didn't drive." It was only a one-year old van but reminded them of one of their favorite cartoons; a group of teenage friends solving mysteries.

"Scooby dooby doo my ass." Sheila paused as she laughed

"Are you sure though? I'm not going to be putting a hitch in your day?" Sheila wanted to make certain.

"I got it, I'm on nobody's schedule today. I'll grab everything and drop it off before surprising Geri and finding out what's really up with her love life."

Sheila handed her the car key fob; Mattie had a key to her home already.

"There's some leftover peach cobbler in the fridge that you can help yourself to, and don't mind the mess, the kids will be cleaning the entire house when they get back in a couple of days and I ain't playing."

Mattie pulled her book bag over her shoulder and hugged Sheila before tucking her necklace under her three-quarter drape top shirt.

The shirt had a logo of the local college football team walking a Wolverine as a pet with a caption that read "Have some of these nuts." The insult was laughable.

Mattie's old pair of flex motion bootcut blue jeans fell over her black calf high boots and Sheila couldn't help but to take a swipe at her outfit.

"I didn't want to say this earlier, but your Lara Croft outfit might be too much today. Halloween is right around the corner; you should save it for then."

Mattie performed a pirouette before responding.

"Now that was actually funny Lala. I'll be back after smashing some cobbler." She finished with a smile on her face as the elevator door opened.

"You just ate half the cafeteria." Sheila yelled out as the elevator door closed.

It had been very difficult adjusting to losing her grandmother and being patient with her aunt. Once Mattie realized that Aunt Penny had lost the last of her siblings, she understood the strength she was witnessing from her elder.

Mattie missed the presence of Grandma Redd.

She waited patiently for any apprehension, but the case to find a suspect lingered. In her heart she knew the possibility was slim, she questioned why she had not installed security cameras on the property. This was something she vowed to remedy.

When she walked onto the level Sheila advised her vehicle was located, Mattie clicked the key fobs alarm to pinpoint the minivan.

Mattie adjusted the leather seats and mirrors when she got in and turned the radio down, as Sheila had a song blasting by Charli XCX featuring Lizzo. It was her get up and go conquer the world song for the day. Sheila's range in music had no limits, she listened to her staple R&B, but Folk

Music, Jazz or Heavy Metal fell well within the range of her friend's listening pleasure.

Mattie laughed and sent a text to Sheila repeating the words of the song "I blame it on your love," before she realized that her friend didn't have her phone.

She put the minivan in reverse before driving towards the exit, waiting behind two vehicles in front of her. As she waited to pull forward, she text Kendal to verify plans for later when he was done teaching a computer class for Frances, who was sick. They had planned to take Frances soup and a small care package to help ease her symptoms.

When she pulled out onto Riverside Drive the sun was shining and she embraced the warmth. She understood life and death was a transition and the only control she had over either was how she lived her life to have purpose. The universe had blessed her with an abundance of love and for that, she was grateful to know she indeed was favored.

NO MISTAKES ALLOWED

The expressway was always less crowded moving away from the downtown area. When Mattie exited Morse Road, she decided to clean out Sheila's van.

She put everything she was unsure of in the rear trunk space. The crayons she found under the seats were mixed in with old French fries and packets of ketchup.

Mattie found two twenty-dollar bills stuck in between the

center console and driver's seat as she vacuumed out the entirety of the inside. She bought an all you can use access sticker and put it on her credit card, paid six months in advance. Kendal confirmed he would be ready to go and check on Frances. He sent a meme of a bouquet of flowers. Simple gestures like this had meaning for Mattie because they were genuine and authentic.

Mattie sped around the corners and curves of Sheila's neighborhood until she reached her street tucked away in an old subdivision near Cooke Rd and I71.

The cul de sac had character. Five properties set equidistant from each other; each house different in design. Mattie knew the neighborhood was perfectly safe for a single mom and children, with both a police officer and city attorney living on the street.

Mattie parked in front of the house because Sheila's driveway still had small puddles of dirty rainwater and she didn't want to mess up the car wash she had selected. She texted Geri to make sure she'd be in the office for her visit and then left her book bag in the car and phone in center console to charge.

"That took planning." Mattie thought as she looked

towards a neighbor's house set up for Halloween. Rows of different colored tombstones frequented the front yard. A wavering ghost was hanging from one side of a tree, while a witch was positioned on the other side sitting on a branch like it was flying on a broomstick. In the shrubs were small mannequin-like figures and gremlins peeking out between the hedges.

The other houses on the street, including Sheila's, had beggar night decorations but nothing close to the house that went all out for the holiday.

Sheila had bought her house right after the divorce, she needed a fresh start. The house was a three-level split. Over two thousand square feet, it had enough room for her and the kids, with ample space for growth.

The same company Mattie used for some of her upgrades in her building had remodeled the new kitchen and bathrooms, while Sheila and her friends painted.

In the end Sheila had a new-found sense of freedom and accomplishment and something she could call her own.

With her nursing salary, alimony and child support from James, she was approved for a much larger mortgage, but

Cindy had advised that she would have instant equity, as she found Sheila the house on a short sale and by removing her profit from the transaction.

The front yard was large enough for two trees and a small garden. The columns at the entrance had floral designs, and the color matched the small white pebbles surrounding Sheila's small bushes.

The driveway wrapped around the front lawn, with another portion that allowed access to the rear of the house where the two-car garage was located, along with a multi-level deck.

Cindy had a fire pit built for Sheila right after she closed on the house as a surprise. The stone surrounding the pit was leftovers from another home improvement project Cindy had taken on, and when all was said and done Sheila had considerable equity in her house within the first two years.

Mattie waved at a person in a car who was pulling out of the adjacent driveway, as a UPS delivery truck pulled in front of Sheila's minivan.

Mattie waited as the driver walked a package towards

her.

"I can take that." Mattie said as the driver handed her a white box.

She recognized the name of the company as one who provided scholastic children's books. All four women drilled into the children how important school was for their future success. These books were pushing the children to read more, with emphasis on the accomplishments of people of color who were so often left out of traditional education.

When Mattie opened the front door, her first thought was Sheila's description of the mess the kids left was an understatement. There were kid's toys all over the floor and bowls of popcorn and containers of juice on the living room table. The trash can had been knocked over in the kitchen, and somehow it was laying in between the kitchen space and dining room.

The cabinets in the kitchen were swung open with broken dishes on the floor and Mattie noticed two large black containers with wheels on them sitting in the middle of the kitchen floor.

When Mattie looked closer, some of the furniture was flipped about with slash marks in them, she knew this was not what her friend had described.

Mattie knew Sheila had been burglarized and reached for her phone, but she had left it in the car, in her book bag along with her gun.

She knew Sheila would lose her mind having her home violated, but first she needed to call 911. Three digits that would never be lost to her.

"This shit is so crazy." She thought knowing the risk taken by the criminals with a heavy law enforcement presence. It made her nauseous to see her friend's house like this. She was even more upset that Sheila had not set her house alarm, especially after her own house had been broken into. She then remembered Sheila was burning the candle on both ends and gave her sister-friend a pass.

Mattie had the sudden realization that the burglars could still be in the house and instead of risking an altercation against unknown intruders who could be armed, she backtracked quietly towards the entrance, keeping her eyes open for movement.

While retracing her steps, she saw one of Sheila's cats first, followed by a woman who was now barring her exit with a knife in hand.

She was a little larger than Mattie and had her face covered with a black skull mask hoodie. She wore black tights and matching boots.

The silver blade glimmered as the sun rays spread through the window. Mattie had seen this style of knife as a child and when training with Roberto.

The karambit was used for close quarter combat, but it seemed to also have been used to rip apart Sheila's couch and love seat.

Mattie wanted to avoid this confrontation if possible and saw no need to risk injury. Being prepared also meant finding means and ways to avoid conflict.

"If you have what you want just go, I don't want any trouble just take whatever you have and go."

Mattie carefully watched the woman's movements.

The tension in the air thickened as the woman walked closer to the front door. Her actions told Mattie that it was escalating and with the woman tossing the blade back and forth between her hands, Mattie determined that this woman knew how to wield it.

The half facial covering only showed her eyes, but her eagerness was seen underneath it. She watched Mattie silently as if contemplating on how to proceed, but when she gripped the handle of the curved blade tightly it seemed her mind had been made up.

Mattie kept her distance, as the woman slowly advanced, but she did so towards the fireplace where she could use the poker in defense. She kicked a cream-colored couch cushion towards the advancing assailant to slow her approach. She knew her best option was distance, along with something to defend against the blade.

Mattie had no idea of the 'why' this was happening, but when the woman jumped over the love seat and advanced; the 'why' was no longer important.

The woman stalked Mattie, who found an area she found comfortable fighting in. Mattie picked up the poker with just enough space to utilize the length of it and stay out of range of the knife.

The assailant jabbed at Mattie testing her, but Mattie knew not to retreat backwards in a straight line; every movement had purpose.

Mattie feinted with the iron rod to counter her position, seemingly startling the burglar followed by what appeared to be a smile under her black facial covering, but that lasted temporarily.

The woman erupted with a flurry of movements, faster than Mattie had expected. Knife in one hand creating a diversion, she kicked Mattie in the stomach, knocking her backwards over the love seat. Mattie scrambled to get up and as she did, she swung the iron rod to slow down the woman's forward movement.

The kick had connected with power and knocked the wind out of Mattie.

The intruder took her time advancing on Mattie a second time, as Mattie regained her feet.

She tossed the knife back and forth again, but Mattie had made that mistake once, she watched the placement of the woman's feet and not the knife.

Mattie quickly understood that the knife was the biggest

threat, but without the proper distance the knife would be ineffective. The woman jabbed at Mattie again. She repeated the last sequence of moves, but Mattie countered by side stepping the kick to raise the poker. She slammed it against the wrists of the female intruder.

The impact was forceful, and the thud meant it connected solidly.

The knife dropped and without haste Mattie kicked it across the room, but in doing so her adversary was able to grab the poker. The ensuing struggle found a surprisingly tight grip on Mattie's arm which made the iron rod fall to the floor.

A sharp elbow to the face brought Mattie's attention back into focus.

"Always be ready" the words flashed in her mind.

Mattie took control of the woman's neck with a Muay Thai clinch and kneed her twice, and as she released the woman, she returned the elbow driving her back. The force caused the half cowl to drop, and Mattie could clearly see her face as the woman tumbled backwards over the long couch.

The surprised look on the attacker's face was quickly replaced with anger.

"I didn't come to kill you, but you're going to die." Those were the only words she said as she slowly closed the space again with confidence in her movement. She assumed that Mattie could be no match for her.

Mattie heard what she said. Clearly, she was sent to kill her sister. This woman was trying to rip apart another piece of her life.

Mattie's anger quickly built, but she had learned angry people made mistakes. In this moment she allowed her muscle memory from years of training to come fully into form.

"I'm going to take that knife and carve your heart out with it. This is my family and you're going to pay for ruining this shit!" Mattie exclaimed closing the distance faster than the woman realized.

Out of pure instinct the woman raised her hands to block Mattie's strike and countered with a blow to Mattie's ribs. The pain from being kicked earlier resurfaced, but Mattie blocked it out and ducked to avoid a second elbow to the face.

This woman was skilled, but Mattie had seen this before; an over aggressive fighter who was eager to overpower their opponent. Mattie was a quick study in each art form she had learned, and in close quarter combat every inch of her opponent was vulnerable.

Mattie imagined the wooden horse she practiced on and struck with the same precision and it drove the woman into the kitchen counter. She then used the same knife combination except with her hands on the woman, finishing it up with a kick to the knee, the woman took the full force of Mattie's kick not being fast enough to check it.

The woman hobbled backwards with instant concern in her eyes. She saw the knife within her reach and tried to move towards it, but Mattie had made that calculation already.

She retrieved the poker and slammed it into the opposite arm of the knee she had just injured.

"Aagh fuck!" The woman screamed, attempting to jump backwards before Mattie connected again. Every instinct told her that this could not be happening. That somehow, she had gone from predator to becoming prey.

No longer was the smug expression shown, no more threats of murdering anyone. She was now fighting against an unknown factor and she was losing.

She grabbed Mattie's arm as she swung at her again. Mattie lost her balance and fell. The woman scrambled on top of Mattie trying to take advantage of the position. She punched downwards at Mattie with a few of the strikes connecting to the side of Mattie's face, but Mattie was patient in this position. She had to be.

Although the woman appeared to have a dominant position, Mattie knew better.

"I'm going to kill you and wait for this nursing bitch to get home and gut her too!"

The woman gained confidence, not realizing that Mattie wasn't simply blocking most of her downward punches but had sprawled up; thrust her hips upwards, while placing her feet on the intruder's waist to pivot her angle. Mattie slipped the woman's punch and latched onto her arm. She locked her legs across and behind the woman's neck and positioned her body to gain complete control.

The burglar tried to break the grip, but Mattie had been patient enough to make sure the lock was in place and then began applying force to the woman's elbow joint.

Mattie could taste the blood in her mouth, and it invigorated her. This threat excited her senses and made her feel alive.

The woman clawed and scratched towards Mattie's face but couldn't reach.

She tried kicking her legs, but with every movement Mattie tightened the lock on the arm bar. Mattie torqued her upper body and added pressure until her elbow popped out of socket, as the woman yelled Mattie released her and crawled to retrieve the knife.

The woman withered backwards, kicking her feet up towards Mattie but it was a futile effort. Mattie picked up the poker and beat her with it until there was no resistance, the blood splattered across the floor with each blow as the woman tried to bargain for her life.

"You don't have to do this, I will leave, and you'll never see me again, I'll never take another job, just let me go." She said agonizing in pain and exuding fear.

Mattie gripped the curved blade knife and tossed it back and forth in her hand as the woman had done earlier.

The energy of aggression raged inside of Mattie, there would be no conflict in this moment because this death would be justified.

Mattie felt the pain in her jaw from the elbow and strikes the woman had rained down on her. She could feel the soreness in her abdomen and ribs. This heightened her senses more than simple everyday practice. Sparring was controlled but this, this moment was life and death and she had been prepared.

"You don't have to do any of this. I'll tell you who sent me." The woman begged, as she kicked up towards Mattie trying to keep distance between them, but her kicks were futile.

Mattie wondered how many times this woman had heard that in her line of work when she took the life of a victim.

Mattie knew this woman was a professional by the way she had just fought back, but with the blood covering Mattie's shirt and face, the only thing she had on her mind was eliminating this threat to herself and her family.

She held the knife in her left hand; and picked the poker back up and began beating the woman again until there was no resistance just a whimper.

Mattie mounted the woman to only stare down at her. She wanted to feel the fear emanating from this woman who had admitted to taking a job to kill her sister.

Mattie rationalized that information was beneficial, but when the woman spit blood in Mattie's face, anger took over and Mattie stabbed her in the armpit; the first deadly blow.

"Had you just been a random act of violence, I'd call the police and let them deal with you, but you threatened someone I love. I told you that I'd carve your heart out."

Mattie plunged the knife through her chest plate, applying pressure until the woman took her final breath.

CHAPTER 14

I'M GOING TO SAY IT ONE TIME...

Sheila was walking towards the nurse's station, after speaking with a patient being released from their hospital stay, when she heard Mr. Harold complaining to the male nurse, he didn't want to care for him.

"No, you can't check shit for me you queer." His tone was adversarial as were his words.

"Mr. Harold you will not speak to any of my nurses like that."

Mr. Harold tried to talk loudly over her, but Sheila cut him off.

"You WILL NOT speak to any of my staff like that. We are here to help you and no other reason. Trust and believe, it is better to have us wanting to help instead of just doing our job. If I hear you being disrespectful again the next week will be a long week for you, you will only get standard care and not the extraordinary assistance we provide." Sheila finished as Mr. Harold calmed down and got the point being made.

"Thank you, Ms. Sheila, I promise I did nothing to excite that man." Norris said as they walked towards the nursing station.

Sheila shook her head, acknowledging that there was no reason to apologize.

"Some people are just like that, don't let people effect your work, and especially not your life."

A man and woman were speaking with a doctor who pointed towards Sheila and Norris as they approached.

"Sheila Patterson?" The female asked showing her badge.

"I am officer Brimmer and this is my partner Officer Holmes. We are here to escort you to our office." She said flatly tucking her badge back under her blouse.

Sheila didn't understand what she had just heard, but she had done nothing and began to refuse the request.

Norris didn't budge, he took up a mock defensive position close to Sheila with his arms crossed. He stood nearly six foot three inches and had blonde hair. If Sheila said she wasn't going they would have to take him along with her.

"Listen I don't think you have the right person, what's this about?" She asked a second time. She knew she had rights and unless she was under arrest she was staying put.

The male police officer laughed at Norris and told him he understood why he was being protective of his coworker, as the female officer pulled out her cell phone and made a call.

"Just like you said, here she is." The woman handed Sheila the phone.

"Sheila, it's Henry and I need you to go with them. They are bringing you directly to me." He said.

Sheila was still in the dark and needed to know more.

"Henry what's going on?"

"Do you remember that nurse, the one my officer was speaking with, the one you said you had never seen the night you got attacked?" Henry relayed the question as Sheila flagged down another duty nurse.

"Yeah, she was new, I think. I haven't seen her since then though." She replied with curiosity in her voice.

"We believe she was the killer's partner, the one that I shot, and she's cleaning up anyone that can identify her. She's dangerous and I need you here, safe. I've been calling you for the past hour, have you seen anything strange or had anything unusual about your day?" He followed up.

"No, not really except Mattie stopped by and had breakfast. She went to my house to get," Sheila paused.

"She shoulda been back by now Henry, that's been almost two hours ago." Sheila urged Henry to get a hold of

Mattie and to stop by her house to see if everything was ok.

Henry spoke back with Officer Brimmer to secure Sheila and bring her directly to the station, while he drove to Sheila's house. He called Mattie on her cell phone, but it just rang and went straight to voicemail. He tried reaching her on Sheila's house phone, but all it did was ring. He was hanging up from one last attempt as he pulled onto Sheila's street.

He saw her minivan sitting at the curb in front of her house and pulled into her driveway.

When he got out of his car, he stepped into a puddle of water, but was unaffected, as he walked towards the front door and peaked through the small windows on each side of the columned entrance. The white sheers deterred a clear view into her home, but Henry could see furniture overturned.

His heart dropped and the hair on his arms straightened. He was nervous, but as he went to kick the door in, he tried the handle first.

He unlatched the holster to his .40 caliber Smith & Wesson, removed it from his hip and made sure there was one bullet in the chamber. The door opened slowly, and as he looked down the hallway towards the kitchen, he saw what looked to be two large black plastic containers.

He walked the few steps into the main portion of the house and was stuck in place.

His eyes fixated on the living room; it was an open space but the ordeal that had transpired cluttered the room. The red splatter on the sofa was sporadic at best. His eyes traveled the small trail of the blood's origin and he found his gun lifting as he did not know what to expect.

Henry saw the woman's dead body with the knife sticking out of her chest and the blood pool surrounding it. He took another few steps into the living room with his gun drawn. He had heightened senses and with a small amount of force he could discharge his weapon quickly if necessary.

The cat's meow made him turn quickly towards the sound and that's when he saw Mattie, sitting in a chair stroking the cat's head.

Henry saw the swollen lip and small cut under Mattie's left eye. Her blue jeans were covered in blood and her dark three-quarter top was stained, but he was relieved that it wasn't her lifeless body laid out on the wood floor.

"I think she came to kill Sheila and the kids." Mattie said as a matter of fact before Henry could say a word. She seemed unaffected by the dead woman's body.

Henry walked towards Mattie and bent down. He looked her over more closely and noticed the scratches on her upper body and neck.

"I'm ok." She made eye contact without showing any offense to his worried face.

"I am pretty sure she planned on stuffing the bodies into those containers, and there's also a small van out back she planned on using," Mattie paused.

"I killed her in self-defense, and because she said she was going to murder Sheila. Who would want to harm Lala?"

She had been sitting in the chair for thirty minutes attempting to answer that question, but she drew a blank.

James, Sheila's ex could be disrespectful and an ass, but Mattie knew he loved her, he simply didn't know how to forget his ego to show it. He was ruled out.

She thought about any beef that her brother Junie could have had with his business associates, but Mattie knew he ran a tight ship with his four distributors and the last thing they would ever do was bring attention to their hustle.

Henry stood up and walked towards the dead body. If Sheila had walked through that door she would've been killed, and of this he had no doubt.

"If she is who I think she is, she was hired to clean up the mess from the hospital. She killed the officer who left his post at the hospital the night of the shooting and was cleaning up loose ends." Henry looked over the body more closely.

"I have to notify the appropriate people, but I'll keep this as quiet as possible." he called his partner Garrett to have him notify the coroner's office and their boss. He advised Garrett to request Jacqueline Sims in the Coroner's office because she had been discreet on several other cases they had worked.

"So, what happened besides the obvious?" He asked Mattie who remained seated. He knew Mattie well enough to know asking her if she was alright would get him minimal response.

"I told her to leave and take whatever she wanted, but she threatened my family and then attacked me. I made sure she couldn't threaten anyone else...ever. I stabbed her in the armpit before her heart." Mattie held no emotion in her response.

Henry wondered if Mattie was in shock but as the conversation continued, he understood she was putting this moment into one of her mental compartments she used to deal with traumatic circumstances.

"I need to take a look around; take pictures and you know I'll have to get an official statement on the record at the station. I'll have you change when a female officer arrives to bag your clothes. I'm sure Sheila has something you can put on." Henry said as he canvassed the rest of the house.

Garrett was first to arrive on the scene, followed by Jacqueline from the Coroner's office.

"Shit." Garrett said when he entered the living room. He stared at the dead body before he saw Henry taking pictures of Mattie and some of her wounds.

"Hey partner, looks like someone got help remodeling." The joke went flat. He walked towards the kitchen and out the patio door towards the rear of the house after Henry told him about the van.

Jacqueline had begun looking over the dead assassin's body. She didn't say a word as she took notes, but the small noises she made were that of disbelief and when she did speak it was matter of fact.

"Time of death is roughly thirty to sixty minutes ago. Cause of death will be determined but preliminary findings show two precise fatal blows; one puncture to the axillary artery and the other through the chest cavity into the heart." She finished speaking into her recorder before turning it off.

Jaqueline looked at Mattie and then around the room. She went to speak with Mattie, but an officer in uniform had entered and been instructed to assist Mattie in changing and securing her clothes.

Henry wanted the least amount of information out to avoid news crews and it appeared he had achieved it.

Shortly after Mattie changed, Henry retrieved Mattie's book bag and phone. They exited the back door as Henry pulled his vehicle to the rear.

It was the first time Mattie had seen the van doors open. It was lined in plastic and had equipment to dismember a body. Her thoughts flash-backed to the human traffickers as she recalled the van, they had intended to use that evening at the mall.

"Thank God you're ok." Henry said as he backed out of the driveway. The coroner had already transported the dead body into her vehicle and was already in route to her office.

"Thank God we are all ok." Mattie replied as she looked at herself in the vanity mirror.

"The universe doesn't make mistakes." He reassured Mattie with her own mantra.

"Indeed."

Mattie closed the vanity mirror and cracked her jaw. She was now feeling the aftermath of being in a life and death struggle. Silently, she thanked God for the preparation her father had played a part in.

A small group of officers had just been briefed on the most recent events when Mattie and Henry walked into the station.

The few stares at Henry and Mattie quickly faded as Shcila walked towards them out of the chief's office.

"You know that's one of my favorite shirts." Sheila said as she wrapped her arms around her sister.

"Wait until you see how I decorated your house." Mattie replied holding onto Sheila as the tears formed in her eyes. She was grateful to be able to hug her friend, to know she had prevented a tragedy and her emotions were coming to the forefront.

Henry directed people around the two women before moving them into a room together. He understood Sheila would require details and he had no reason not to ask Mattie questions on record with Sheila present.

Mattie went step by step from the moment she had entered the house.

Henry was audio recording the interview as Garrett and the captain watched from behind the two-way mirror. Paulette, the Assistant District Attorney joined them and listened with detail to Mattie's account.

Henry concluded the interview and told them Sheila's house wouldn't be available as they investigated. He left the room to return with 20oz. bottles of Pepsi for the women. He then departed again to join the others behind the mirror.

"I wouldn't want to get on her bad side." The captain said out loud to no one in particular.

"All of this stems from early summer shit, and the two assassins sent to clean up are dead. No little league organization hired them. Someone with global reach brought them." Garrett said.

Henry knew that his partner lacked pride in his appearance and even drank too much, but when it came to detective work, he had a keen mind.

"I have a scheduled call with Nickels' attorney at three o'clock. I will do whatever I can to get more information to you guys. I wouldn't want to get on her bad side either. Be successful Detectives." Paulette finished before exiting the room.

"Counselor." Henry bid her farewell before the Chief interjected.

"There are storm clouds forming at city hall, and although this will be a big win for us, until we find out who murdered the Mayor's friend's nieces the shit will continue to roll downhill. It would've been better to have one of them left alive." Captain Turnkle added before Garrett spoke up.

"One of them alive means some of us would be dead sir."

Henry agreed and walked out of the room and that's when he saw Geri and Cindy sitting at his desk. He pulled them back into the interview room with the other two friends for privacy, because he understood emotions were running high. He turned off the video recording as the four women consoled each other through tears and jokes meant to lighten the mood.

As Henry watched through the mirror, he felt his eyes water too. He wiped them before returning one last time to see if they needed anything before they departed.

When he walked into the room, he realized how close this dynamic had been to being ripped apart.

"You guys, you're like my sisters and I love all of you." He left the room a second time to call Paulette on logistics. He wanted to be present at the time of Nickels interview. Captain Turnkle released Mattie and reminded her she may be needed for follow-up questions.

Kendal met them at Mattie's house when he got the call
from her. She told him the short version until they were
face to face.

She would say it once for everyone and hopefully be
done with it.

Kendal knew people who had traumatic episodes in their
lives and often remained in shock, but as Kendal spoke
with Henry on the phone driving to Mattie's house his
concern faded.

"She's been through so much in her life, those areas most
people have conflict she keeps black and white. Once
something is justified in her mind it's rarely an issue for
her. Her concern was for Sheila and the kids."

Geri and Cindy were sitting on the couch when he walked
in. The news was on and a brief story about what transpired
had just faded on the screen.

Sheila and Aunt Penny were sitting at the dining room
table having a glass of wine.

Mattie walked out of her bedroom in long cotton pant

pajamas and a black tank top. She walked to Kendal and hugged him a little longer than normal. She took him by the hand and led him to the dining room table before calling her two friends sitting in the couch.

Mattie told the story in detail, leaving nothing out.

She felt it necessary to share the unadulterated truth, it was the only way to have fewer conversations about it in the future. When she was done, she asked them as a group and individuals to not act differently because it would be a constant reminder of what she had come to terms with.

Aunt Penny agreed with Mattie and advised the rest of the group that if she caught wind Mattie's request wasn't being met, they would have to deal with her. She then relayed that she loved them all for the first time before walking away.

"That woman." Mattie felt the same energy of protection that Grandma Redd had exercised. Mattie excused herself to speak with Kendal privately.

"When they're done investigating, I need you to put her house back together exactly as it was before this mess. Geri and Cindy are going to try and put new shit in and make it better, but Sheila will need everything back to normal, or as close as possible. They're going to stay here tonight and tomorrow night with Cindy." Mattie finished.

"Ok, but honey how." Kendal attempted to ask before Mattie cut him off.

"I am fine, just kiss me."

Without hesitation he did.

"I'm tired but not sleepy are you staying?" She asked before making her way to the door.

"Is that a trick question?" He asked rhetorically.

"I'll grab ice for this." She pointed to her entire face and mustered a grin.

Kendal slipped his button-down shirt off and kept his undershirt on. When she returned, she kissed him again, placed her head on his chest and fell asleep.

MY BROTHER'S KEEPER

Kendal woke early to finish the final bit of the winter programs being offered. He was sitting at the front activity desk when Mattie walked into the center. He was surrounded by a few students and Frances, giving each other high fives.

"Hi, Ms. Parks." Toya noticed Mattie before anyone else. She had been stapling volunteer sign-up sheets for an upcoming car wash fundraiser to be held before the weather turned cold.

"Good afternoon young queens and kings, what's with all the joy?" Mattie asked. Kendal stood up from behind the desk when he saw her to approach.

"We have funding for the next two years and we may even have enough for an addition to the building to update the pool and exercise areas, we just have to maintain a ninety percent graduation rate for anyone accepted into the program." Toya answered with a huge grin on her face.

"Ms. Parks, such a pleasure to see you." Kendal said kissing her on the cheek in front of the students.

"Are you serious?" Mattie excitedly jumped into him so she could hug him. This was the first good news she had heard in such a long time and she needed it.

"Yeah she is dead serious. They were impressed with the proposal, the few things that you changed around in it made a gigantic difference, and with the success of the kids improving in their class work we may be onto something here." Frances interjected.

"I can't believe that you're in here today. You're feeling better I see." Mattie reached out for the older woman's hand.

"Between the city and church donations and now this, these kids have a real opportunity at better lives." Kendal added to the conversation.

He looked at Mattie and wondered if she was prepared to answer his question on slowing down to heal.

"And yes, after everything that keeps happening, I'm going to take a lot more time off from work to get my head right." She already knew what he was thinking after their conversation the previous evening.

"Who is it honey?"

Kendal winced as he stared at his phone.

"It's Kwame." He said flatly. He led Mattie into his office as he let the phone keep ringing to go to voicemail.

Mattie noticed her picture on his desk when she walked in and she felt wanted.

With the loss of Grandma Redd, it felt good having someone in her life, someone who had sacrificed the past few weeks to make her his priority.

"Baby, I want you to accept their offer, you'll be gone for

a little bit and I can come here and help out while you're gone. This is your passion and I'll fly in a few times if you want me to, it won't be sooo bad."

Mattie knew that she was going to miss him, but she wasn't selfish.

"Baby you don't think it's too soon considering everything over the past weeks?" He looked down at his phone to see if Kwame would leave a voice message.

"Honey, I'll be fine, Grandma's passing still hurts, but each day gets a little better and yesterday is in the past. I want you to live your dream. It's your purpose and I love you, so just do it."

Mattie walked over to the edge of his desk where he was sitting down in his chair, mustering up strength to pretend she didn't have issues with it.

Kwame was calling him again and before he answered the phone, he wanted to make sure she was ok with it. He was having mixed feelings wanting to protect Mattie, but he knew she could take care of herself.

"Are you absolutely sure baby?"

"Yes, baby I'm sure, now answer your damn phone man!" she said nudging him on.

"Yeah count me in." He answered.

Mattie could hear Kwame in the background, and he was excited too.

Kendal gave Kwame the fax number to the center to send over the scheduled dates and locations of the tour. Kwame sent it immediately, so Kendal walked out of his office to retrieve the list.

Mattie sat down in his chair and started spinning in a circle. She thought about how the day had gone so far, all the extreme decisions she had found herself making since she had met Kendal.

"At least I have a couple more weeks with him before he leaves." She thought hoping that would be her blessing to keep Jimmie Fredericks off her mind. She still believed he needed to be taught a lesson, a lesson his parents failed to teach him twenty some odd years ago, treat people with respect and don't hit women.

Kendal's calm demeanor kept a certain level of peace around even when the storm raged, with the one exception

223

of him pushing the male nurse into the desk, but even then, he apologized after the fact.

"Baby," Kendal walked back into his office. It was the way he said it that Mattie knew something was wrong.

"What's up honey?" she spun the chair back to face him.

"Well, I got the schedule and the good news is we'll be in Charlotte and Raleigh for the week of my nephew's birthday. Oh, and the other good news is that tour kicks off at the Apollo theatre in New York City." He paused again and then leaned forward to hand her the schedule.

Mattie took it with a questioning smile on her face. Her eyebrows initially raised, but as she began reading, she squinted as she saw what he was talking about, the not so good part. He had to fly out the next Friday.

"Damn, that soon. I thought it was still a month out or so. That's from the information from Geri's interview with Patricia and Kwame last week, she said the dates were going to be listed in the magazine...humph." Mattie felt dejected.

She placed the schedule on the desk, sounding more frustrated than what she had intended.

She grabbed an ink pen and marked off certain dates she would fly into the city the tour was performing. Carolina was definite, she was going to meet more of his family, and she'd probably spend most of the time with his mother.

Atlanta was also definite, she had college teammates in ATL, San Antonio, TX and San Diego, CA were marked off, and she would make Kendal show her his old apartment. All in all, there were twelve more cities, but Mattie hadn't narrowed them down.

"I'll be at these. I'd come the first weekend, but Aunt Penny is still gon be here." Mattie nervously put her hands in her pocket. She felt the butterfly knife and gripped it unintentionally.

"Yeah it's much sooner than I had expected. The Apollo Theatre is going to be bananas. Sammy Davis Jr., Bill Cosby…" Kendal was excited.

Mattie interjected,

"Bill Cosby, really?" Once her role model and America's Dad from the television series, she was still uncertain of what to feel for his entire ordeal as others stripped him of his iconic status.

"And Michael Jackson have performed on that stage. I'm going to have to work late this week and my only request is that we fall asleep and wake up together. I'm gonna be jonesin' like a crack fiend." Kendal approached her to look at the dates she checked off.

"You know make sure that if you decide to fly out to some of the other places that you let me know in advance and I'll get a bigger room for us to share. Kwame told me on tour, the rooms are cramped and there are usually two to a room to cut down on traveling expenses." A knock on his door interrupted his thought.

"Mr. Scott, excuse me, but do you have time? I can come back if you want me to." Alonzo said standing in the doorway.

"Come in Alonzo." Mattie instructed as she stood up from the chair.

"Honey do you want me to bring something back for dinner. My surprise of course." She said touching him on the hand.

"Well what do you think Zo, we'll probably be here for a while, should we get pizza or chicken?" Kendal asked

Alonzo.

"Uh, Mr. Scott, they both sound good but I think Ms. Parks said it was her surprise."

Both Mattie and Kendal laughed out loud, and the younger man had a grin on his face.

"Yeah, I guess she did say that, so Ms. Parks to answer your question, yes please bring us something back of your choice. Alonzo is allergic to seafood so cross that off your 'surprise list'.

He excused himself from Alonzo to walk her to her car, he opened her car door and she kissed him; once more rubbing her hand up against his crotch.

"Just making sure he's alright too. We don't want him to feel left out." She closed her car door behind and rolled her window down.

"I'll be back around six, six thirty, I'm going to run to the courthouse."

She was madly in love with this man and felt a deep connection between them.

Mattie vowed to make sure Kendal got all his nourishment to be at the top of his game while on tour, this was his time and she was going to support him to the best of her ability.

Mattie wasn't sure if she wanted to cook when she entered the courthouse to check on her foster brother Sam, who was now represented by Clayton Monroe III at her behest.

In a sense, Sam had an impact on her life as he always believed there was 'right' and there was 'wrong' regardless of what the law said. After she read various statements on his case, it was clear that the plain clothes cops who entered Sam's house intended to rob him and they had. They had not identified themselves until after Sam beat him with a bat, per the audio recording left on accidentally by one of the officers. The prosecution had failed to provide this bit of information earlier and now Sam's attorney was using it against the city prosecutor.

Clayton had sought a continuance after getting Sam released on bond.

When the judge said, "released on own recognizance", Sam smiled scanning the courtroom and saw Mattie as she walked out.

She turned to look backwards, and their eyes met, he shook his head affirmatively recognizing there was at least one person in his corner after the life he had been dealt.

Mattie decided to make a detour when she left. She was anxious as she measured the conflict in her head about James Fredericks. Now that she had had a taste for blood, her reasoning wasn't as clear as she would like.

She purchased Ribeye steaks for Kendal and Alonzo, to prepare with garlic mashed potatoes and Brussel Sprouts sautéed in bacon grease. Mattie hoped that her showing resolve in her daily activities would prompt Aunt Penny to leave sooner, but she wasn't going to actively rush her out of her house.

She was family and now the Matriarch, so she was due respect, Mattie just prayed to get some respect in return.

A text message came through from Grace advising her to once more take the full twelve weeks of bereavement.

Mattie thought back to Jimmie Fredericks for a third time, she had pictures of his house fading in and out of her mind as she drove home from the store.

As Mattie walked back into her house with the groceries in her hand, Aunt Penny was coming from the patio taking off yellow rubber gloves.

"Your neighbor dropped off an envelope, slid it right under the door. It's over there." Aunt Penny pointed to the counter.

Mattie opened it and it was the rent check. She thought about correcting her aunt about saying 'neighbor' when it was her tenant, but in a sense, they were neighbors and she didn't want to get in any type of argument from such a small misnomer.

"I'm going to grill some steak and make a few sides auntie, and tomorrow I'll cook some wings for you."

Mattie pulled a medium sized glass bowl along with two pans from her cabinet and the seasonings from the pantry.

Aunt Penny had put all the cleaning supplies away and asked Mattie to wake her when the food was done. She also informed her niece that she needed a ride to the shopping center to get yarn, she was going to finish the blanket her sister had started for Kendal.

"And if you really don't know how to crotchet yet, I'm

going to teach you before I leave." She shook her head affirmatively as she walked down the hallway towards the guest room.

"Yeah right." Mattie thought putting her seasoning mix on the meats.

Her grandmother hadn't gotten her to learn and she highly doubted that Aunt Penny would do any better regardless of how adamant or tough she wanted to be about it.

When the food was done, she put two containers together to deliver back to the center to help nourish both Kendal and Alonzo.

CHAPTER 16

MORE THAN

The next week flew by. Mattie spent most of the time with Kendal at the center, helping him by lending a hand to Georgeanne and Skip; two of the new faculty personnel.

She planned on spending a considerable amount of time at the center to stay busy, giving the illusion to Aunt Penny that she was sticking to a routine. Her aunt had been more open to spending time with her niece.

Mattie was able to set an appointment to see Dr. Stevens.

She spoke freely about taking another life. He reinforced her resolve in understanding her justification. The struggle for Mattie was the fine line between self- defense and something else. Her only regret was not controlling her emotion in gathering more information before killing the female assassin.

When Mattie left her appointment, she knew any contemplation of regret in taking the female intruder would never surface. She would do it all again for any of her family.

Geri and Cindy had been busy all week. Sheila and the children were staying at Cindy's house while their home was being put back together.

They had not shared what happened with the young ones. It was agreed by all, they didn't need to know.

In a sense everyone was on edge dealing with their own ambitions drove the hectic energy during the week.

Cindy was closing two deals and had to be diligent in making sure the paperwork for both properties was immaculate, because her client was purchasing both homes for her family. If one deal fell apart so would the other.

Geri was adding the finishing touches to the next edition of "Under the Sun". She updated the tour list and added a picture of Kendal into the article. She had received multiple phone calls from the group in Chicago about sitting back down with them. They wanted to share new terms once she turned down their original offer.

Geri decided to build and declined secondary terms as well. She would take her own path by gaining larger following.

Kendal spent both Wednesday and Thursday night practicing his pieces.

First, he recited them in the mirror before having Mattie as his one-person audience. Mattie saw what Kwame had mentioned about Kendal being 'unique,' it was in his perspective of life and the world.

"My day has been long. Aunt Penny broke down and cried today. She shared so much with me and then I couldn't help but cry with her. I'm drained and tense at the same time." Mattie set down on her couch after throwing her keys on the kitchen counter.

Kendal had packed for the tour earlier so he could spend the last bit of time with her before his departure.

"That feeling can be overwhelming and I'm glad you two had your moment together. I'm going to take care of you tonight, and I'm pulling one of your moves. No talking unless I let you. Deal?" Kendal smiled and held his hand out for her to shake.

"When does this deal begin?" Mattie leaned over and kissed him.

"The moment you walk into your bedroom. While you dropped the kids off to Sheila, I took the liberty of setting a peaceful environment; so as soon as you walk into your bedroom the deal begins, until I say."

Kendal extended his hand again.

Mattie was curious and walked towards her bedroom door.

"Deal." Mattie shook his hand and opened the door.

When she entered her room, Mattie was taken aback. Candles were lit and spread throughout her room creating a dim luminance.

Mattie saw oil being heated on a small table next to a massage table Kendal had set up.

He had a merlot colored sheet neatly folded at the end of the table with a small pillow situated on top.

"Baby, this is so," Mattie had forgotten the deal they made.

Kendal slapped her firmly on the ass.

"Shhh." Kendal held his index finger to his lips and smiled.

Mattie shook her head in agreement. She would follow his instruction and not say a word unless he gave her permission.

Kendal walked to her dresser and retrieved a card.

"For you."

Kendal kissed her cheek and then walked into her bathroom.

Mattie opened the card and began to read it as she heard the water hitting the tub from the shower head.

She smiled at him when he walked back into the room and turned the space heater on medium.

Kendal kissed her on the other cheek and placed the card back onto the dresser before undressing her. He kissed her clavicles and neck and then led her into the shower.

The water temperature was perfect as it hit her skin. The streams of hot water always relaxed her, and it was exactly what she needed. Her day had been an emotional rollercoaster with Aunt Penny, and then with Sheila having lingering thoughts of what transpired in her house.

Kendal lathered a washcloth and began to wash her body while sharing how sexy she was.

"That feels so good." Mattie was in mid-sentence when Kendal slapped her backside. forcefully.

"Umph." Mattie jumped and looked at Kendal.

Kendal added more soap to the water and began washing her again.

"You have to ask for permission." Kendal leaned into the shower attempting not to get wet.

Mattie felt a new sensation as she asked for permission to speak.

"May I speak Sir."

Kendal let a smile cross his face.

"Of course, you can beautiful, you can do anything, almost anything tonight if you ask properly."

Mattie had never allowed anyone control like this. She didn't trust the men in her past to express this desire.

"That stung a little."

"So why are you smiling?" Kendal asked

"Because I liked it Sir."

He rinsed her body off and then towel dried her from head to toe. Leading Mattie from the bathroom he had her lie flat on her back on the massage table. A white sheet was placed over her body up to her neck.

Mattie was surprised that the sheet was warm. Kendal's attention to detail had not gone unnoticed.

"No words, unless." Kendal said firmly.

"Stress can build from top down or bottom up. I want to start around your temples and work my way down."

Kendal took a small bottle, situated next to the massage oil and allowed a few drops into his hands. He lightly began massaging her temples all the way down her face and back up around her hairline.

Mattie's eyes glanced at the candles flickering in the background, she felt the rise and flame in each one as

Kendal touched her with a light touch.

He skirted the sheet further down beneath her breasts to get to her clavicles and shoulders. Never once allowing his hands to retreat from her skin except to gather more heated oil.

Two drops fell between her breasts and towards her belly button. His hands covered the areas between her chest and her stomach. He touched every part of Mattie's body except her breasts. The expectation of feeling his touch on her nipples made her excited.

He peeled the sheet back further and massaged her hips. He traced her pelvic bones with two fingers with enough pressure it made Mattie inhale slowly. Her body tingled on the entire side Kendal's hands touched.

"I know what you need. I'll get every bit of this tension out of you. You deserve it baby."

Kendal pulled the sheet to one side of her body, splitting the sheet directly between her legs. He touched every inch of her leg, rubbing the knots out that she didn't know had accumulated.

It was a pleasure pain moment when he pushed harder than intended on her second leg.

"Umph." She exclaimed

"Was that too hard?"

"Yes and no Sir." Mattie moaned a second time as Kendal applied slightly less pressure in his fingertips.

"Turn over."

Kendal helped her flip on to her stomach.

The muscles in her back flashed, but it was the mark on her shoulder that stood out. The smaller blemishes had mostly faded, however the gunshot scar remained.

He started at her feet and worked upwards.

Again, touching every inch of her body with one exception.

The small oil beads being rubbed in, along with the slow deliberate pressing upward and back down her calves had Mattie enjoying the exertion in his grip.

Her hips lifted off the table feeling a jolt of energy run up her spine.

"Umph."

She lifted her hips attempting to guide his fingers into her heaven.

Kendal took her hands and placed them at her side.

"Don't think about anything, just relax."

He moved back up her body from her lower back to her shoulders. Kendal added more oil and took his fingers and traced her spine down to the small dimples in her back and then back up again.

"That's giving me goosebumps." Mattie let out.

Kendal slapped the other cheek more firmly.

"Mmm, I'm sorry Sir." Her body wiggled from the heightened sensations coursing through her body. She was being turned on by relinquishing power to him.

"I know you're used to keeping things pinned up, but right now you have no thoughts or concerns, you have no worries simply inhale and exhale."

Kendal covered her body with the sheet as he retrieved a dark bag from beneath the massage table. He kissed her on her back and took a step back so Mattie could see his movements.

He opened the bag; pulled out medium sized silver clasps, four in total. Oval shaped, they looked sturdy.

Mattie wasn't sure where this was heading, but the curiosity kept her gaze on the next items.

Kendal closed the bag and walked around the table tracing her body with his hands.

"I belong to you and you belong to me."

Once he returned to her line of sight, he reached back into the bag and pulled out new packs of nylons and laid them across her bed.

Mattie watched him.

She had never imagined following a man's lead like this. She had never submitted to another, but because of the trust in him she was willing to meet her submission in the power she was allowing him to have.

Kendal poured out the last two items into the bed so that Mattie had a full view of each item. The black eye covering didn't surprise her, but the red ball gag with black leather straps was pleasantly surprising.

"Are you ok?"

"Yes, I am sir."

This, was introducing a different aspect to their romance, exposing himself, leaving no stone left to be unturned.

Kendal gave Mattie water to drink while he fastened the silver clips into placements in each corner of the massage table. Each time one latched, he kissed Mattie's body closest to where the clasp was placed.

He opened the nylons, cutting them into smaller pieces to thread through the silver fastenings, only to wrap the other ends around each ankle and wrists.

"Are you deserving of everything I want you to have?"

Kendal moved towards her bed.

"Yes, I am Sir." Mattie could feel her legs trembling simply thinking about what was happening. How she had let go of fear to submit to Kendal; to explore a deeper part of their sensuality. Kendal bent down and pulled her goody bag from beneath her bed and her eyes lit up.

"I didn't think you knew."

As soon as the words passed her lips, he thumped her back with an open hand.

"I'm sorry Sir."

Kendal pulled out Mattie's massager and plugged it in the power strip.

"You deserve to have all that pent-up energy released, don't you?"

"I do Sir." Mattie shook her head affirmatively.

Kendal kissed her again and turned her over onto her back to lay.

"I have your permission." Kendal asked as he picked up the blindfold covering.

"Yes Sir." Mattie answered as he tied the covering across her eyes.

Kendal added more oil to her body and began to massage her again. This time he was more deliberate when touching her. The initial massage had been a release of tension, now there were other releases to be imagined.

He took her legs in his hand and began kissing her feet, while massaging her hips with his other hand. Mattie tensed as her toes found their way into his mouth and his fingers found the way inside of her sweetness.

"Oh god." Mattie exclaimed and immediately Kendal slapped the inside of her thigh making her body twitch.

"You have permission to say yes and my name only."

"Yes Kendal." Mattie moaned as he switched his attention to her other foot. The restraints pulled on her extremities each time energy shot through her body and knowing she had no control turned her on.

Kendal slowly moved his lips up her leg while tracing the other leg with his hand.

Mattie felt his lips and tongue on her skin creating goosebumps. One hand moved to her breasts, the other the inside of her thighs.

"I love the way your skin feels, the way your skin tastes. I see it excites you too."

His observation was an understatement, her nipples hardened from his touch. She let out a moan when he kissed the top of her vulva.

"Yes Kendal." Mattie's breathing became erratic each time her flesh was touched.

Kendal walked around the table, intermittently touching and kissing her breasts and shoulders.

"Ask me to help keep you quiet Madison." Kendal needed to make sure she still held no reservations as he picked up the ball gag.

"Please Sir."

"Open up."

Kendal placed the mouthpiece inside and fastened it around her head. He kissed her on the cheeks and then he poured more oil across her skin. He undressed and brushed his body against her hands, which dangled at the side of the massage table.

"You can touch me."

Mattie's hands reached out for his body, but he stepped towards the bottom of the table to allow his manhood to touch her feet.

He walked to her bed and grabbed her electric massager, placing it right next to her ears and turned it on.

The sound of the vibrations made her bite down on the covering in her mouth.

Mattie was startled and her body jumped again.

Kendal massaged her with one hand as the device followed behind. The goosebumps frequented each portion of her body that he touched.

Down one side of her body and up the next. He kissed her stomach while changing the speed of the massager as he used it on different body parts.

Mattie's body twitched each time an androgynous zone was stimulated, and the restraints kept her from moving when the sensation was too much. She had lost control and it excited her.

Kendal began sucking her nipples as the massager found itself between her legs, pressed up against the entrance of her wetness.

Mattie's breathing increased while the moans seeped through her.

"Oh god." She forced the two words through the red ball.

Kendal kept his mouth on her nipples while his hand still controlled the massager, but with his other hand he pulled Mattie's hair tightly and she let out a loud moan.

He removed her eye covering before walking to stand at her side. He began kissing her stomach downward until his lips were laid across her heaven.

He pushed her thighs further apart until the massager was fixed beneath his mouth. He turned the device off; with his tongue he traced it across the petals of her flower while massaging her breasts.

This side position allowed more of her clitoris to be stimulated than the typical straight on position. The sensation had forced the last bit of her control out. The gag pressed against her mouth was being loosened with each moan indicating that her arrival would soon be met.

Kendal turned the massager back on and it overwhelmed her. He continued to massage her breasts but with his other hand he slipped his fingers inside her, keeping his lips pressed between her legs.

The stimulation of the massager and his fingers forced her cavity tight, and the small contractions spread all the wetness onto the sheet on the massage table.

Her body tensed and Kendal firmly slapped her breasts and at that moment the wetness inside of her squirted outward.

Mattie began to scream through the ball gag.

Not wanting to wake Aunt Penny, Kendal placed his hand over her mouth, which intensified Mattie's back to back orgasms.

Kendal turned the massager off and removed the restraints and black leather straps holding the red ball.

He kissed her forehead as she whimpered, and her body trembled.

He kissed her passionately before lifting her off the massage table.

"Hold on honey." He wiped off any excessive oils before he helped her into bed.

"I can't, can't believe that happened, that I let that happen." She said softly reaching for his manhood.

"Can I have some more?" She stroked him and kissed his chest.

"Mattie, I belong to you. Do with me as you please."

Mattie fulfilled Kendal and they both fell asleep hard. They had one more session when they woke up, and then once again before taking him to the airport that afternoon. She held back any tears when he went into the waiting area alone.

They talked on the phone until his plane boarded.

Mattie decided to go back to his condo to get the rest of her clothes and laptop.

As she pulled out of his neighborhood, a phone call from Geri was coming through.

"What's up, you and your man have been busy this whole week, you get everything done you needed before he flies out? Don't hit my shit, you see I'm already in the lane!" Geri was yelling at someone out her vehicle's window.

"Just pull up some," a second woman's voice was heard in the commotion.

"Damn, what the hell are you doing Geri?"

Mattie was grateful her drive was not as hectic as Geri's was sounding.

"These people act like they can't drive; this chick was trying to bully me. She don't know she can get these hands." Geri laughed loudly before she finished,

"Did you drop your man off yet?" Geri asked ignoring the people around her.

"Yeah a few hours ago." Mattie answered.

The disappointment could be heard in Geri's voice.

"Fuck, I had two copies of the magazine hot off the presses to send with him. I'm going to go to the gym tonight to kill myself and you're going to meet me there. Afterwards me, you and Cindy can go get a drink or two. They got live reggae playing down in the Short North somewhere tonight mon."

"That's cool, I got workout stuff in my trunk, just washed some clothes at Kendal's. What time you want to meet at the gym?"

"About seven, in a couple of hours or so." Geri paused

"What station are you listening to? I keep hearing that song everywhere."

It was a new joint by Gov White, originally from Cleveland, Ohio, but now living in Los Angeles after getting his first real break.

"WHOT." Mattie answered.

"That song is choppin em. I'll see you at seven and I'll

call Cindy in a little, so she'll know the plan, bye mama." Geri hung up after Mattie said goodbye.

Mattie didn't want to go home just yet and she didn't have much time to go shopping.

She looked at the exits coming up on the expressway. She was only two exit ramps away from the Hillside neighborhood.

"No, let me just take my ass on home." She tried to talk herself out of getting off at the exit.

Mattie forced herself into the fast lane thinking that would help deter her, but the other voice inside her mind was telling her to get off, so she veered two lanes over and exited.

"This is crazy." She said out loud as she pulled into the parking lot of The Deuce. She didn't have her gun, but she had her butterfly knife in her jacket pocket and her pepper spray on her key chain. She decided to move her car and park closer to the flea market and grocery store on the other side so people couldn't see what she was driving.

Mattie crossed over the alley she had driven down on Monday when she first came searching for the bar. She pulled her hair up into her hat and threw her sunglasses back on to hide her face.

As she walked into The Deuce, she took a mental inventory of everything. She remembered the billiard tables and dart board from her first canvas, but what she couldn't see from the outside was a decent sized dance area. The stage was built into the far end, with a state-of-the-art sound system and a stationary DJ booth.

The advertising for the Halloween party was situated throughout the establishment.

"What's up with you momma?" An older white woman with wrinkles under her eyes was the only afternoon bartender at the time. By her demeanor Mattie could tell that she had been around the block a couple of times.

A few people sat around the wooden bar countertop drinking out of frosty mugs, while two men shot Eightball on the pool table.

"For starters, where's your bathroom luv?"

Mattie wanted to scan the place further and ensure that neither of the men from the corner store were present.

"Straight back on the other side of the dance floor."

The silver streaks in the bartender's hair were more noticeable as she pointed in the direction of the emergency exit.

Mattie did have to pee, but she wasn't going to do it in an old dusty neighborhood hangout spot.

"Ain't no telling what's crawling around in the bathroom." She had been in other establishments like this. She could hold it because her bladder wasn't going to burst.

"Ruby, where's our brew baby girl?" One of the men shooting pool said in a casual tone as Mattie walked into the bathroom and to her surprise it was very clean. She decided she had enough information that she didn't have to waste any more time. She walked out of the restroom and noticed that the emergency exit didn't have an alarm.

"That's just stupid and weird." She walked back and took a seat, ordered a Corona so she wouldn't be remembered as the bathroom lady if she did come back for the Halloween party. She watched Ruby open her beer before acting like she got a text message.

"Damn, I completely forgot that I gotta drop my people at the Greyhound."

It provided her an opportunity to leave without causing attention. She put a ten-dollar bill down on the counter and stood up making sure she tipped the woman.

"You don't want to kill this first?" Ruby asked her as she started walking away from her stool.

"Naw just ditch it or give it to one of these guys, but I gotta go." Mattie quickly walked out the door.

When she got back to her vehicle, she started shaking her head and laughing at the same time. She amused herself that she had gone earlier in the week to please her curiosity, and now she was entertaining the subtle whispers in her mind.

Jimmie Fredericks had been the one talking about paying her a visit at work, but she was out doing him. She had already been to his house and now his neighborhood business.

"That was so fucking crazy." She turned her radio up as she drove away.

"I'm not going back for the party. What the fuck would I do anyways, cuss him out and get into a fight in front of a whole group of people? That wouldn't be smart. People would know it was me, and he would know it was me." Mattie kept coming up with all sorts of reasons why she shouldn't go back, but she still hadn't found an adequate one to appease the other appetite that desired being fed.

"I need to look different *if* I go back." Another whisper sounded in her mind. It wouldn't be difficult as costumes were welcomed for the Halloween party.

Still with a forty five-minute wait before their workout, Mattie found herself pulling into a different small strip mall just a few blocks away from the gym. She decided to stop at a beauty supply store that carried a multitude of items.

She thought about coloring her hair as she walked into the store, but wasn't ready to make such a permanent change.

Two younger Asian women were behind the counter. One was assisting a black woman with a scarf wrapped around her head trying to direct the girl who was pulling packages of hair off the wall. The customer interrupted her for a third time.

"No, no the Yaki #2."

The other woman was sitting on a stool reading a hair magazine with a grin on her face, as she kept looking up to scan the store.

Mattie decided against coloring her hair and opted for buying three different wigs. She started to pay for them with a credit card but that other voice began pushing forward, telling her to pay cash.

"Leave no trace."

When she got back into her car, she looked at herself in her rear-view mirror and asked the same repeated question.

"What am I doing?"

A question to which the answer would have to wait, because a picture of Cindy flashed on her cell phone.

"What's going on hooker, you ain't sporting Kendal's clothes and shit are you now that he gone?" Cindy asked laughing through the speaker.

"Whatever, I ain't got his clothes on but I got something

of his inside of me." Mattie replied laughing as hard as her friend had.

"Oh my God, too much information, just way too much info. Geri text me talking about reggae tonight, you know Sheila gon be pissed. I got some 'fire' for tonight."

Mattie was grateful normalcy was returning to their lives.

"So, we will meet you after we are done working out?" Mattie was close to the workout facility and needed to end the call.

"Nope, at the gym." Cindy said quickly seeing if Mattie was really paying attention.

"At the gym?'

Mattie wasn't sure that she understood what Cindy had just said.

"I am going to the gym too, I didn't stutter."

"What? My gym, I mean, me and Geri's gym?

You joined?"

"About three weeks ago, we didn't want to say anything

until I had a few workouts under my belt, Geri said you would try to kill me. I'm pulling up now so see you when you get in here."

CHAPTER 17

TRADITIONS

After a short time listening to reggae, Mattie found herself laying on the couch talking to Kendal about his flight and hotel.

They talked until three in the morning, when she forced him off the phone so he could get some rest. She fell asleep on the couch, only to be wakened at six in the morning by Aunt Penny who had begun brewing coffee.

"You can't stay up with the owls and expect to get up with the early birds." Aunt Penny relayed as Mattie slowly sat up and stretched her arms above her head.

"Huh?" Mattie responded not fully comprehending what her aunt had just said.

Aunt Penny poured two cups of coffee and then sat down next to her on the khaki colored leather sofa.

"You can't be burning the candles at both ends." Her elder paused to take a sip.

"Have you thought about going back to speak with your doctor Madison?" Aunt Penny asked regarding her psychologist. Mattie tended be hesitant discussing Dr. Stevens with anyone, but she had accepted Aunt Penny's concern being genuine, like her grandmother's had been before.

"I'm still seeing him auntie; I just saw him a few days back."

Mattie sat up to look for where her cell phone ended up after her conversation with Kendal last night.

Mattie, at times, still expected to see her grandmother

walking down the hall, but the fact that Aunt Penny was sitting next to her was a constant reminder that her grandmother had passed.

"Fine, that's fine. Later this morning we gon pick up some flowers and go visit the burial. I want to be there before eleven, and then I need more yarn from the fabric store since you're going to learn how to crotchet real soon, once I'm done with this blanket Amy started for Kendal." It seemed the elder woman's agenda was set in stone.

Mattie thought it an excellent idea to visit Grandma Redd's grave and put fresh flowers on it. She would have fresh flowers delivered to the site weekly.

The other part of her aunt's plan wasn't going to fly. For one, she wasn't no old woman that needed to pass the time away by sitting in a chair with a needle and yarn; secondly, she hadn't let her grandmother teach her and Aunt Penny wasn't her grandmother and thirdly,

"Thirdly I just don't want to do it." She counted each one silently before she responded.

"That's a good idea auntie, we can see if the floral shop will take a credit card to have flowers delivered every week." Mattie stretched her arms and legs once again.

"Just give me a couple of hours, I need to lie down for a bit more first, then we can visit her. She'd like that."

Mattie stood up and walked into the kitchen. She opened the refrigerator and pulled out a 20-ounce bottle of Pepsi and took a sip.

"And after we leave the burial, we're going to the fabric store. Amadahy told me you were stubborn, but every woman in our family knows how to do it. We couldn't always buy clothes, we had to make what we wore by stitching fabrics and crocheting blankets and the sort; so, you can ignore me or pout about it, but you are my niece and you're gonna learn before I leave." Aunt Penny said as a matter of fact. She wasn't being aggressive, just stating a fact.

Mattie stood by the kitchen island contemplating if this was the moment she was going to have the first real adult conversation with her aunt on how to respect people's privacy and wishes, and to let her aunt know that she wasn't the boss of her. She thought against it because it wasn't even six thirty in the morning yet.

"I'm going to lay down auntie, I'll be ready by ten thirty." Mattie said walking out of the kitchen and down the hall into her bedroom, closing the door behind her. She laid on the bed wondering if she should call or text Kendal 'good morning', but decided it was still way too early and he was probably getting the last few sheep counted before starting his day.

The sunlight was making its way through her bedroom windows and Mattie watched the small dust particles swarming around in the rays of sunlight. She tried turning away from the windows and fluffed her pillows to get more comfortable, but that didn't help.

She sat up in her bed, propping her back against her headboard and then reached into her nightstand for the remote to her audio system and turned on WIIOT for their weekend morning show.

She looked to her long dresser and saw the bag with the wigs she had bought. Mattie found herself picking up the bag and walking into her bathroom.

She bought one short wrap styled wig, a long blond wig and a medium length sandy brown wig with curls in it. She also purchased a long black wig she thought Geri would

269

love.

She put the blond wig back into the bag.

"Too obvious."

She replaced it with the brunette short wrap-style
wig. She walked to her closet and pulled out a leather
miniskirt, long black boots and a multi strap black top to
see if it was enough to change her appearance. As she
looked in the bathroom mirror her appearance was altered,
but she realized that a miniskirt would be the last thing she
should wear.

She changed the skirt for some black leather pants that fit
her slightly loose in the waist and kept on the black top.
She exchanged the longer boots for shorter ankle boots that
left her enough room to attach an ankle holster without
drawing attention.

Mattie examined her outfit.

It was better, but the wig didn't hide her face as much as
she would've liked. She swapped it out for the curly sandy
brown wig and got a vastly different look and energy. Still
not satisfied, she went back to her closet and rummaged
through hats, finding an old black leather cap she had never

worn.

"Now that's more like it." Thinking the only thing left was to put on makeup. It was a Halloween party, so she planned on resembling Gamora from Guardians of the Galaxy, with a little hood flavor.

"Hell no, nobody would even know it was me." She looked older and with the leather outfit fitting loosely she didn't have much of a shape. Mattie figured that *if* she was going to pay The Deuce a visit, she had the perfect disguise, especially for a Halloween party.

Mattie undressed and opened her curtain to let more sun in before sitting on the side of her bed. She was trying to formulate a game plan on how to get Jimmie Fredericks away from the nightspot without him leaving with her. Every plan that she came up with entailed exchanging phone numbers so she could tell him to meet her somewhere. She would need to let him think that he was gaming her and that his personality was getting him another so called 'player' for his team.

"There's no way he, or Ruby for that matter would recognize me."

There was no other way except to exchange numbers to get him out of the little night spot without her at his side.

"Fuck."

She realized that she could simply purchase a prepaid phone from a store 'down the way' and pay cash to activate it without giving her information to the salesclerk.

Mattie shook her head up and down realizing that she had just put two parts of the Jimmie Fredericks' plan together.

"Sick, just sick." She was amazed that she had even thought that far about teaching a low-grade thug to threaten people or abuse women. Perhaps the near life and death fight was tilting the balance, but now wasn't the time to push the thought. Mattie felt tired suddenly and laid back down feeling drained. She fell asleep until she heard Kendal's ringtone sounding off on her cell phone.

"Good morning, beautiful woman of mine. You're still laying down from the sounds of it." His voice was upbeat.

"Hi baby, no I'm up. I mean I was up at six this morning talking to my aunt. I just came back to my room for a minute. How'd you sleep, what time is it? Mattie felt better hearing his voice.

"It's almost ten o'clock baby and I slept ok. I kept waking up off and on thinking about you. Honestly though, I am a lot nervous cause I'm the only one that doesn't have major performances under my belt. A couple of artists toured with Kwame over in Europe last year and," Kendal said but Mattie interrupted

"Baby don't go psyching yourself out, you'll be fine. This is what you want, and your purpose can't change without God's permission. So, don't worry. I miss you so much and Aunt Penny had one good idea and one bad idea." Mattie paused to yawn and stretch her arms.

"The good idea is to visit Grandma Redd today. I'm going to have a floral shop deliver fresh flowers every week too." Mattie swung her legs off to the side of her bed trying to get her mind and body moving together.

"And what was the bad idea?" Kendal asked

"Yeah, the bad idea is to teach me how to crotchet because all the women in our family can do it, because back in the day, they had to make blankets and clothing and…" She kept going on before Kendal cut her off

"Ok, baby I got it." He sounded amused

"But before you get all MMA with Aunt Penny and be having 'rumble in the jungle part two' take your time and think about learning. It just might be a good tradition to pass down to our kids, especially if we have a girl one day." He said casually.

Mattie was aware now and internalizing what he said, but still wasn't convinced that she had a good reason to learn; but having a child did mean she would have to be the first teacher.

Mattie, for the first time in her life, hadn't balked at the idea learning how to crotchet.

"Yeah, I hear you Kendal Abraham, so how many pieces do you get to perform, they're going to be recording all of them, at least that's what Patricia said in the interview with Geri?" Mattie assumed in a questioning tone.

"I'll get twenty minutes, and you won't believe the response we have here in NY. The radio shows are blasting it and today's art section has a picture of Kwame on the cover. Stephen and Patricia put a lot of money into this and from people calling the radio stations asking about tickets, they're thinking about adding an extra show for Monday night, since we don't have to be in D.C. until

Thursday." Kendal asked Mattie to hold on while someone spoke with him in the background.

"Baby I've got to go, we're about to have a walk through and then head down to a radio station for an interview. I'll call you later and I love you very much." They hung up after Mattie told him she loved him too.

Mattie heard Aunt Penny start the dishwasher and looked at the time on her cell phone.

"10:14." Mattie realized she had roughly sixteen minutes to shower and dress if she didn't want to hear her aunt's mouth.

"She gon say the wrong thing one of these days."

Mattie stood up to pull out a bra and panty set before walking into the bathroom to take a quick shower and brush her teeth.

Aunt Penny wanted the windows down so she could feel the air against her face when they headed towards their destinations; Mattie wanted the air conditioning on, so she opened her sunroof and put the AC on. A good compromise she thought.

When they walked into the flower shop, the fragrance of fresh scents lightened both of their moods.

The older woman at the floral shop hesitated as she took Mattie's credit card information after telling her she would have to pay for two months in advance with an attitude.

Mattie didn't like the way the older woman had talked to her, being short with responses when asking pertinent questions about weekly deliveries. Mattie pulled out her Platinum American Express Card and Driver's license and told her to charge one year in advance, and the woman's demeanor changed.

Mattie played along with the change in attitude, but it was Aunt Penny who spoke plainly to the woman.

"You ought to be ashamed of yo self, judging people before you know something about them, the same way we got judged and picked on, you better than that."

Mattie was handed the Ocean Breeze Orchid bouquet, bought to take with them to Grandma Redd's resting place.

The older black female clerk was shocked and didn't know what to say as they walked out except 'my apologies and thank you for coming'.

Mattie and Aunt Penny arrived at the cemetery, there were two internments going on. Mattie hoped that Aunt Penny didn't relapse and have an emotional fit, because she didn't feel like carrying her back to the car.

Aunt Penny was using her wooden cane, so as they approached the grave site, she pointed her cane towards the tombstone, which had two bunches of flowers on it already.

Mattie bent down to read the cards with the flowers. One set was from Sheila's kids and the other from her three friends.

"She was right, them women love you." Aunt Penny said placing their bunch of flowers next to the others. Both women stood before the grave thinking, taking a moment to reflect.

"You know she's very much like me Amy, smart, stubborn...sassy...all the things you used to call me. Funny how you were the youngest but always the most mature, and even though you didn't think I listened to you or took your advice; yours always meant the most. I know sooner than later I'll be up there with all the rest of y'all. I'm just about finished with what you started and when I'm done, I will be teaching our niece how to crotchet. Now I know you said it was virtually impossible, but nothing is impossible. I miss you Amy...I miss you." Aunt Penny asked Mattie to help her bend down.

She kissed the top of the grass around the tombstone before Mattie helped her stand back up.

Mattie bent down and repeated what her aunt had done.

"I love you too." She said before standing and walking back to the car.

"You ready to run me by the fabric store?" Aunt Penny strapped her seatbelt on as Mattie started her ignition. Mattie paused trying to come up with a good excuse but couldn't find any.

"Yeah, yeah I guess auntie." Mattie said pulling out of the gates of the cemetery.

Mattie looked out the corner of her sunglasses at her aunt, who was looking out the window like she was smiling at someone.

CHAPTER 18

RATS EAT ANYTHING

Mattie sat at the end of the bar sipping on a Corona. She watched the young woman behind the bar open her bottle and walk it to her, for some reason she felt a heightened sense of awareness which came with a bit of paranoia.

She read about bartenders slipping drugs into patron's drinks; setting them up to be robbed, raped or kidnapped, and with Jimmie Frederick being among the crowd right now she wasn't putting anything past anyone. A bouncer stood at the door checking people for weapons. As Mattie had thought, he only touched her waist to check before allowing her in earlier.

Jimmie was already in the back near the DJ booth sitting at a table with a woman wearing sunglasses. The woman wore heavy makeup and an Afro wig and large hoop earrings. She resembled Pam Grier from Foxy Brown.

"You want something else?" The bartender asked.

The evening bartender was wearing blue jeans and a dark red T shirt. She stood about five foot six inches, but she was thin, very thin. She wore large framed red glasses and a Santa hat.

Her shirt read "Santa's little helper."

"If you got dem winning lotto numbers." Mattie made light talk in the moment.

"I'm straight for now, naw let me get some ice. I gotta pace myself. The DJ gon start spinnin' it in a minute tho right?"

The night club had a decent amount of people, both pool tables were taken, and other people were playing darts.

Some of the costumes were tacky, but a few people had taken care in their appearance.

Two men dressed in Men in Black suits were throwing darts, and another couple were dressed like characters from the movie Black Panther.

Mattie's attention was drawn back towards the entrance to two women speaking loudly with each other as they walked in. They made eye contact with the bartender who began making their drinks immediately.

Mattie wondered who they were and why the doorman didn't pat them down.

"It's about to come down like a muthafucka out in that bitch." One of em said, drawing Mattie's attention out into the parking lot.

"There he go right there." The younger of the two women motioned to where Jimmie was sitting.

The younger woman wore short blue jean shorts and a bikini swim top.

The older woman wore a black miniskirt with a halter top. They were heading towards Jimmie's table when the younger one frowned at Mattie.

"I don't know what that bitch lookin' at." She told the older woman who simply glanced at Mattie before placing her attention back on Jimmie.

Jimmie was now accompanied by a light skinned man wearing a plain black cap. His gold fronts could be seen every time he smiled or laughed at what Jimmie was talking about.

The two women slowed at the end of the bar to secure their drinks and then continued along their trek.

"I got money." The older woman said.

"I might have enough." The younger one added, before sitting at the table behind Jimmie waiting until he was done doing his business.

Mattie could hear Jimmie talking, brokering the deal for his 'employee'.

"You light homie, forty dollars don't get you shit with this one, but hold on." Jimmie slid out of his booth to sit down with the two women sipping their drinks at the table behind.

"What you hoes got? It ain't even midnight, so why the fuck y'all in here anyways. This party ain't for y'all asses." He said counting the money from each of the females.

"What the fuck is this Jewel, a hundred and forty fucking dollars, today is trick or treat and you ain't doing good at either." He intensely stared at her.

The older woman had a little more than three hundred dollars, so he didn't say much to her.

"I'm gonna get you more when it stops raining." Jewel said.

"When it stops raining, it ain't raining out in that bitch right now is it?" he asked reaching over to touch her shirt; she jumped backwards expecting to be hit.

"What the fuck!" he grabbed her by her wrists aggressively.

"You know what Jewel, you gon make me some cash right now."

He went back to the other table to make a new deal.

"My man, dig this, she my moneymaker right here." He hesitated to put his arm around the woman, who hadn't moved from where she sat waiting on him to return.

"And you just don't have enough loot for her, that's it, the bottom line." Jimmie said leaning forward.

"But this young broad right here, Jewel." He called out and the younger black girl with braids stood and walked over to his table.

"Yes daddy." She knew she would have to make it up to him to minimize his abuse later.

"I want you to take my homie out back and show him how inexperienced you are." Jimmie told her.

The light skinned man adjusted his black cap and licked his lips, figuring he was getting a bargain, because Jewel was young, under twenty and a physical specimen.

"Fifty dollars and you don't have no time limit with this one, bust one and you done tho son." Jimmie held his hand out for the money to be placed in his hand.

"Yeah, yeah, that's whas up." The man with the black cap was visually excited.

"Oh, and if you hit her, I hit you." Jimmie revealed his shoulder holster with a semi-automatic under his black suit jacket, he lifted his green hoodie to reveal a second handgun on his waist.

"I'm gon beat that young shit up partner, keep that shit covered up tho. This is business homie." The male stood up and followed Jewel out the emergency exit.

Jimmie motioned the older woman over to his table.

"Mel tell that bitch to make em stronger, and what you got left?" Jimmie asked the older woman. He wasn't talking about money, instead he wanted the remaining cocaine left in her dispenser.

Mel handed him the device, who in turn gave it to the other female at the table to take a bump before he did.

"Go grab more drinks." He motioned to Mel who found a spot standing next to Mattie, who had been listening to the whole deal going down.

Melanie flagged the younger bartender down.

"Candy, he wants the rest of em stronger baby."

Candy poured a drop of soda in the glass and the rest Hennessy as Mel talked to her.

"Tell me if this is strong enough." Candy offered Melanie the glass of Cognac and a Bud Light smiling back at her.

Melanie looked at Mattie and then walked back to the table, taking Jimmie his drink.

Mattie continued with her water and beer, mixing them slowly so she wouldn't get a buzz, a trick she learned in college.

She saw Jimmie checking her out throughout the night, casually at first. He was a predator, and a single woman making small talk and having a drink by herself was adequate prey.

Mattie sat on the bar stool with her back angled to their small booth so she could be as inconspicuous as possible.

Jimmie said something to Melanie as she handed him his drink and beer.

"That's how I like it, you know that bitch is getting her ass whooped right, bitch gon bring me some chump change. She think this fifty is part of her stash." He laughed uncontrollably. Mel laughed with him nervously.

"She acts like you did, but I got yo ass in order."

Mattie sat at the wooden bar on the stool, listening to Jimmie. She felt her heart rate increase. Her desire was to crack him in the head with the bottle, but she was also feeling upset in her stomach. She had felt strange all evening once she had gotten off the phone with Kendal wishing him good luck before his performance.

She would've sworn that Candy slipped something in her drink had she not been watching her every move when it came to her beer and water.

"Just my fucking nerves, calm down and breathe." She waited for Jimmie to make the first move because she needed to be the one in control.

"Maybe I'll walk by and look at him when I go to the bathroom." She thought, wondering if her stomach would settle down as she rubbed it. She caught a glimpse of herself in the mirror.

She was wearing the outfit and wig she picked out that morning and her makeup aged her and hid her identity.

"I just gotta calm down."

Melanie stood up again and walked back to the bar by Mattie's barstool.

"Candy, hey Candy. I need two more." She yelled.

Candy was at the opposite side of the bar serving beers and a mixed drink to a couple at the other end.

"Think she heard me?" Mel asked Mattie out of the blue.

Mattie saw the whole request for more drinks ordered, but acted like she wasn't paying attention.

"What's that?" Mattie asked turning slightly to face Mel.

Mattie wore glasses to help complete the disguise, and she found it weird to be self-aware looking through the glasses at Mel.

"Aw shit, nothing ya know, just trying to get a couple more drinks to feel good." Mel responded as Candy came walking down to their corner.

"We need two more of those and two Bud Lights. What do you want?" Melanie asked Mattie.

Mattie figured Jimmie was using this approach to feel her out.

"Naw love I'm good, but thanks." She turned down the offer, hoping it would force Jimmie to play his hand and approach her himself.

"That's cool, just trying to be cordial. I got you if you change your mind."

Mel motioned for the other woman for help carrying the liquor order.

Mattie was finally able to see what the woman really looked like. She was shapely and busty with a thin waist, she seemed attractive, but now that Mattie could see her face, the sunglasses didn't cover everything. The woman had bruises on her face and what looked like a black eye. Her lips were still swollen and the closer she got to the bar, Mattie could see the cuts and scrapes on her arms and hands.

"So, this is the chick." Mattie surmised that this was the woman on the other end of the phone line that day.

"She could do better, what the fuck happened that got her hooked up with that piece of shit?"

Mattie pushed her half empty Corona bottle away and fumbled around with her phone.

Jimmie stood up to let the women sit back down and then approached Mattie, leaving both women at the table.

"You coulda made it easy on me by accepting the invite to let me by you a drink." He said leaning onto the bar to take notice of Mattie.

Mattie slowly looked up at him hoping he didn't recognize her. From the look in his eyes she could tell there was no recollection.

"How's that, you haven't asked to buy me a drink." Mattie replied taking her eyes off him to the people at the door trying to shake the water off their coats.

The bouncer had them take off their coats while he patted them down. The rain was getting in as the door closed slowly behind them.

"You see those two, we're all together so when she asked you if you wanted a drink, she was speaking on my behalf, we're like family."

Jimmie was putting the charm on. He was doped up from

the way his pupils were dilated, and she smelled the drugs creeping through his pores.

He made her skin crawl. From this close range she could smack him open handed against his eardrum and damage it, but she was still unsure what she was going to do, if anything at all.

"I thought she was trying to holla at me, that's what most people are doing when they buy someone a drank." Mattie said just enough to give him room to wiggle his grimy little maneuvers. Mattie glanced at the table and noticed that the woman wearing glasses was agitated.

"Is she upset?" the thought felt like a gut punch. Jimmie was paying her more attention now and the woman was getting upset about it.

"Sick, just fucking sick." Mattie thought wondering how she had been trapped with Jimmie and watching her anger that he was speaking to her at the bar.

"Yeah fo sho, I feel that sexy lady. I'm J. Fred so let me buy you a drank or something." He finally took a direct approach.

"Fuck, tonight ain't that night." Mattie thought, forming

her next move.

"What's yo name foxy?"

Unintentionally his gun flashed under his jacket, but Mattie was dismissive about it.

"I'm Sissy." Mattie paused to place her phone on the counter.

"J. Fred, I'm gon have to take a rain check, I've been driving all day and I'm exhausted. You got a number I can hit you on, actually take my new number." Mattie said, writing her number down on a napkin after reaching over the bar counter.

"Well hold on shawty, how you gon know it's me calling and is the real number, don't be trying to play J. Fred fo real." His true nature had surfaced, and the aggressiveness was heard in the tone he took just like when he threatened her on the phone.

Mattie took that as a cue to head to the restroom while he added her number on his phone.

"He's a fucking childish moron, did I give him the right number? Fucking grown ass clown." She thought as she opened the door to the bathroom.

Unlike yesterday, the restroom was trashed.

Toilet paper was hanging off the side of one toilet and the other toilet was not flushed.

Mattie looked around and decided that none of this shit was worth it. She would leave out the back door and walk to her car without anyone knowing. She had already paid for her beer, so the worst-case scenario was Jimmie calling and leaving messages until he got the picture.

"Let them silly broads fend for themselves, yo dumbass is up in this filthy ass spot, stomach all fucked up." She pulled her prepaid cell phone out as it vibrated from three missed calls; all from Jimmie. Mattie had memorized his information the first day he had threatened her while on the phone at work, so she recognized the number.

"Creepy persistent."

Mattie pushed the lever down for a clean paper towel to open the bathroom door. She put her head out to see if anyone was watching, but what she noticed was a tall guy with two bags in his hands walking towards the DJ stand with big headphones draped around his neck.

The back-door opening startled her. It was Jewel returning without the man.

"What?" She asked Mattie as they passed nearly bumping into each other.

"I'm sorry." Mattie apologized not to make a scene. She had determined previously that smacking Jewel would make no difference in the grand scheme of things.

Mattie opened the emergency door and walked down the few steps onto the pavement covered with almost two inches of water and deeper in other areas.

One of the dumpster's lids was open allowing it to be filled with the rainwater, while the other one was closed, and in between them was an old dirty mattress with wet newspapers spread across it.

"That's some nasty shit. Oh my god." She shook her head in disgust.

Mattie was glad she wore boots as the water began backing up in the alley, she walked carefully not to step on any hidden objects, remembering what it looked like prior to this.

The door opening behind her didn't alarm her; it was the splashing sound before hearing Jimmie's voice saying, 'hold up'.

By the time Mattie turned around he was already bearing down on her.

"You think I'm a fucking idiot bitch, and you can sneak out the back trying to play J. Fred." He smacked her with the equivalent force of a punch.

Mattie saw at the last minute that she was about to get hit and rolled with the force of the slap. She fell on one knee and tried to get up, but she got kicked on the side of her body where she had been injured earlier against the hired assassin. The pain returned, but not as acute.

Jimmie stood over her feeling the effects of the cocaine and Cognac.

"That fucking number ain't real bitch, you tried to play J. Fred!"

Mattie was dazed and seeing two of him, she knew she had to do something because his intentions were to hurt her, but her head was still spinning. She felt a sense of betrayal like the night her father was lost in the darkness.

"I'm gon show you what I do to bitches that try to lie to me, I'm as real as it gets bitch. You gon learn tonight Sissy, if that's even yo real name. If you don't do a good job, I'm gon shove this pistol right up your shit and pull the trigger. Now welcome to my hood." He touched his gun holster.

"I swear to you nobody will find you til Monday. The fucking rats and whatever is out in this muthafucka will crawl up yo shit after I blow a hole in yo cavity. I was trying to be nice in there," He paused as he unbuckled his belt, the rain pelted downward with only a worn canopy overhead slowing it.

"Offering to buy you a drank and shit, you gon give me a fake number and try to dip on me."

Mattie was near the dumpster trying to pull herself up as the water covered her hands. She felt glass cut her.

She wasn't going to be able to get to her ankle strap in time.

"Now instead of having a drink on me, you gon get me right. Bring yo ass over here!" Jimmie aggressively took Mattie by her head.

Mattie felt something on the ground something she could

use; metal…jagged metal from a broken fire escape.

"What da fuck?" Jimmie yelled when the hat and wig came undone. He held it in his hands and staggered.

"So, you're a fucking wig wearing trickster. Well no more tricks except getting me right or I'm shoving something else in you."

He reached back down to grab her to put her on her knees in front of him in an assuming position.

As Mattie was being moved, she felt the slight loosening in his grip as he lost balance from his intoxication, and that's when she sprung forward with the metal rod in her hand.

Jimmie saw it, but he was too slow reaching for his gun. His awkward movements made him stumble into the closed dumpster, but it was too late.

Mattie struck him directly in his diaphragm and pushed upward.

His expression showed he was injured. He desperately reached out for her and stumbled.

Mattie knew the way he fell with his back against the dumpster that she hit something vital. She moved closer to watch him choke.

Mattie pushed the rod deeper into him. She put him into the same category as Ronald Jackson.

"You don't belong on this planet with us, you're a cancer to the human race James Fredericks, you deserve far worse than this." She said, tasting the blood in her mouth from when he attacked her.

Mattie watched him gasp; she relived the night her father attempted to force himself on her and thought about her grandmother's assailant. Jimmie Fredericks was paying for his deeds and the deeds of others.

"Who, who the fuck are you?" He forced out in between coughing and wheezing.

Mattie looked him squarely in the face while adjusting her glasses. She bent down and pulled the wig and hat out of his hand.

"I'm the beyotch in the store on Monday, the same stupid fucking bitch you threatened on the phone when you was whooping up on Ms. Low Self Esteem in there."

Vengeance was the only emotion in her eyes. She held a smirk on her face waiting to see the moment J. Fred realized who she was.

"Monday." He coughed again and fell to his knee. His expression showed that he recognized the voice.

"Yeah that's right, Madison in Columbus."

Jimmie Frederick's eyes lit up and he tried to draw his gun from his holster as one last stand.

Mattie, now with her full faculties, saw what he was doing before it happened and simply punched him in the throat, crushing his larynx. He fell to both knees and onto his side.

She pulled the metal rod from his body and washed off all the blood before shoving it down the sleeve of her leather jacket. She put the wig and hat back on her head and straightened it the best she could.

Mattie looked around to make sure no one had seen what just happened. She took his phone from his suit coat and dug out the napkin with her number from his pocket.

"No, the fucking rats will eat away at you til Monday,

you fuckin' piece of shit." She made her way through the rising water back to her car with her adrenaline still raging.

CHAPTER 19
AUNTIE

"Sorry I'm unable to answer, leave your name and contact information and I'll return your call at an opportune time. Enjoy."

Mattie heard Kendal's answering machine going off, waking her up from her deep sleep. Why he didn't simply add voicemail to his home phone account hadn't mattered until this moment.

"Hey this is Geri and Cindy, Mattie…Mattie are you there?" Cindy's voice came through loud and clear.

Mattie rolled over to grab the house phone to stop the message being left.

Kendal's California King sized bed was fluffed up with comforters and pillows. It was comfortable, but it was a pain to navigate as she looked for the handset which wasn't on the base.

"I don't think she's there." Cindy's voice was heard, speaking to someone in the background.

"Call her cell phone again." Geri's voice followed sounding concerned.

"Mattie are you there?" Cindy asked again before the call ended.

Mattie finally found the house phone mixed in with her leather pants and shirt from last night on the floor.

"Hello…hello…" Mattie said dryly into the handset.

"We been calling, are you ok?"

They were still concerned how their friend was able to

manage losing Grandma Redd, and the physical and mental strain from the fight which left a professional hit woman dead.

"Yeah...yeah, I'm fine. I just finally got a good night sleep." Mattie said, focusing on the digital alarm clock built into the base of the phone.

"Yeah, so everything's ok. We called you for church before going by your house since you ain't answer your phone. Aunt Penny rode with us, we told her you were sick. But back to the question at hand, why aren't you answering your cell phone? It's almost twelve o'clock, you sure you're ok?" Cindy asked again, it was unlike Mattie to be so hard to get a hold of.

Mattie reaffirmed that she was doing fine as she felt her face; which was sore. Her bottom lip was swollen slightly and cut.

"Auntie was concerned, not upset." Geri was telling Mattie after taking the phone from Cindy, who was slightly over exaggerating.

Mattie saw the wig and hat lying on Kendal's bathroom floor and then her eyes traveled to the leather jacket and metal rod resting on the floor.

"Damn I did, didn't I?"

Mattie was not feeling one bit remorseful about what she had done to J. Fred. He struck her first, was about to rape her and possibly even worse.

"So, what if I went there, fuck him. He deserved it." She rationalized.

"It was raining so hard last night, I tripped over something left in the street and hit my face after drinking a couple of beers and a few shots by myself last night. I just had to let my hair down, by myself." She added while hearing a beeping noise on the floor under the clothes she had worn.

"Y'all can swing by here if you want. Does Lala have to work today?" Mattie asked, bending down to move the clothing around to find the source of the chirping. It was Jimmie's cell phone.

"Yeah, she gotta work until four; she's covering for that nurse that helped when Grandma was, well you know. But anyways, Sheila's been blowing your phone up. We're still taking Jay, Darian, and Samantha to the zoo after leaving this cesspool of kids at Chuckie Cheese, so no we won't be swinging by there." Geri laughed.

Mattie yawned and sat up on the edge of the bed and then laid back down.

"Well let me find my cell phone and call her back."

She rolled over, slid down the bed and walked into the bathroom.

Jimmie's cell phone was going off again and as she checked the log, there were over twenty missed phone calls and forty text messages. The last text that came in read:

'Man, I found out about all that shit from the beginning of the summer and we will talk about it but right now I need to know where the fuck are you, people saying that the cops found a body behind the bar in the alley, call me back." The signature on the text was from Big Bruh.

Mattie surmised it was a family member, but still she didn't feel any emotion about J. Fred being slumped over lifeless.

Mattie saw the napkin with her number on it next to the wig and flushed it down the toilet after ripping it up, she then picked up the metal rod and wig and carried both to the garage where she parked her car, knowing that the street had flooded before. Once she found the toolbox, she grabbed a hammer, removed the sim card and bashed the cell phone into small pieces, before wrapping the remains in newspaper.

She took the hedge trimmers and cut the wig into at least sixty smaller pieces, before putting the contents into separate paper. Mattie then retrieved two separate plastic grocery bags and placed the components in each.

Walking back into the condo, she put both bags and the metal rod by the garage door so she could take them when she left.

She heard Sheila's voice message being left on the answering machine.

"Damn, I missed her again."

Mattie walked into the kitchen.

She was hungry and thirsty, luckily for her Kendal went shopping just in case she stayed over at his place while he was gone. She grabbed the package of English Muffins and a bowl of fruit. Instead of her usual morning soda fix, she brewed coffee. As she ate, her lips tingled with pain when she bit into the strawberry preserves spread across her muffin.

"It was either him or me, and damn sure wasn't gon be me." She said out loud staring into her coffee mug.

She powered up the television.

The weatherman gave the forecast for the upcoming week and in the ensuing segment, there was no mention of the murder.

Mattie walked her plate into the kitchen and rinsed it off. She took another sip of the coffee and poured it down the drain, before putting the cup and the plate in the dishwasher.

"Damn, damn…damn, he's probably been trying to call me too." She ran back to her car in the garage to get her cell phone. All three of her friends had texted her at least four times, and Kendal out did them by two texts and five phone calls.

As she sat at the dining room table getting ready to call him back, the midday anchor woman's voice caught her attention.

"The crime rate has been increasing more slowly over the past two years than previous years, although the numbers this year haven't been tallied yet, major crime has gone down over three percent according to a recent study done on the State of Ohio. This summer has seen an increase in the homicide rate, although other crimes are declining. The city has fallen victim to yet another homicide overnight. A man's body was found in an alley behind a favorite local bar on the Southside. The body, just now identified by police as James Fredericks, was found brutally stabbed according to a source close to the ongoing investigation. No suspects or persons of interest have been named; as always we will keep you updated throughout the broadcast." The anchorwoman finished.

"Our prayers and wishes go out to the family who has seen a tragic loss of life this year, law enforcement is still attempting to put the pieces together." Her male co-anchor added.

"If you only knew." Mattie thought back to being assaulted and almost viciously raped.

"That asshole was heavy handed, at least he won't be hitting nobody else." She said out loud as her phone rang.

"Hi baby, Yeah I'm fine. No, I'm at your house, I wanted to smell you, so I stayed. It's been raining badly here, and I slipped and bruised my face, but I'm ok, a little scrape or two...I miss you; how did you do? How was the show Mr. Unique Talent?" she asked excited to hear his voice, but lonely without him. She pushed last night into an afterthought.

"You slipped...?" He attempted to ask.

"Baby, I'm ok...tell me about last night."

Mattie would rather be listening about his night than hers.

"It was so...so fantastic, I wish you were here, one of the poets had to leave because his son got hit by a car. His son is ok, he just called Blue to let the rest of us know to pray for his family. With that strange shit happening, I got a whole thirty minutes instead of twenty. Baby the audience showed us love. I did your poem and all the ladies were like aww." He started chuckling.

"I bet they was like aww, I'm glad his broad ain't here. Don't have me come up there and cut somebody."

Mattie was laughing with him, but some of what she was saying was true, she was possessive of her man and nobody was going to fuck with her happiness.

"Baby if anyone gets out of line and disrespects you, I'd be cutting em right with you." Kendal added.

"I left muffins and food in the fridge and since you're there go look in the pantry, I also left you a surprise." He made her walk into the pantry with him on the phone.

"Ok, I'm here," she said.

A teddy bear with a two liter of Pepsi nestled in its' arms was sitting on a huge box of Hershey's Chocolate Kisses.

"Oh baby…" Mattie felt like she could cry.

"The Pepsi is for that ascorbic acid addiction you got going on; the teddy bear is to sleep with while I'm gone and every time you think of my lips you have a kiss." He sounded just as excited.

"Baby I love you so much. I love all of it, hold on." Mattie scanned down at her phone again to see it was Sheila calling her again.

"That's Sheila I'll call her back when we're done." Mattie said as an afterthought.

"Actually baby, I gotta go but don't be leaving your cell phone in the car. This is the only way I can get a hold of you. There are two more shows Monday night and one added to DC already. Be careful I don't want you using your aunt's cane...I love you." He said before she hung up.

Mattie felt better already, but she still felt nauseous from last night.

"The beer must've been old and stale or something." She walked back up the stairs to make the bed and straighten her mess.

Mattie folded her leather outfit and blouse, putting them in one of Kendal's gym bags. She threw the leather hat in it too.

She called Aunt Penny to make sure she gave her an update, and to tell her she'd be home in a few hours after going to the gym.

Mattie was anxious still. She slipped on some shorts and a sports bra with a tank top over it.

She turned off all the lights, making sure every door was locked, before putting both the gym and plastic bag, along with the metal rod in her car. Closing the garage door behind she thought about her mother, if she would have approved of what she had done last night.

Mattie looked over at the metal rod and decided to dump it.

She pulled over to one of the drain grates and dropped it in, while checking to make sure no one saw her do it.

She needed gas so logically she thought to dump the other two bags in the trash; but decided against 'both', and dumped the second bag with the cell phone pieces into the dumpster at the gym before walking in.

Mattie got on the treadmill after working her arms and shoulders and noticed that Sheila had texted her twice.

"Woman you ain't gon keep ignoring me, having me blow up your phone like you owe me some money. Geri said you were at ya man's house and I called there. I gotta tell you something, call me back." The first text read.

"Call me soon mama." The second one read.

Mattie turned on Pandora, the music application she used on her iPhone and set the treadmill on 7.0 miles per hour.

She thought about Ronald Jackson, The Widow and
Jimmie Fredericks, and how none of them escaped her
wrath. There was no remorse or regret. Thirty minutes later
she was drenched from head to toe with sweat.

The sweat made her lip hurt, and she was feeling the pain
on the side of her head where she had been struck by one of
Jimmie's rings.

Mattie waited to take a shower until she got home. Aunt
Penny was sleeping so Mattie closed her bedroom door and
undressed. She felt the cut on her hand as she turned the
shower knobs; she stared into the mirror and saw the
bruise.

"I'll cover that with make-up."

After getting out of the shower, she put on some gray
jogging pants and a shirt Kendal had left.

"I miss that man." Mattie would spend the rest of her life
with him all he had to do was ask.

Her cell phone ringing made her run into the kitchen.

"Don't yell at me, I left my phone in the car and went to
the gym, and to be honest every time I went to call you

back something came up. I promise you." Mattie was
trying to explain to Sheila before she got fussed at.

"Whateva, I don't' care about that. I been trying to get a
hold of your ass because I followed up with the hospital for
you."

Mattie had received voice mails from the hospital about
an urgent matter. Mattie just figured it had something to do
with the insurance for Grandma Redd's stay and
treatment. She didn't want to stress about it anymore and
asked Sheila to handle it.

Mattie leaned over her bathroom sink with the water
running, brushing her teeth with her cell phone wedged
between her ear resting on her shoulder.

"I wanted to tell your ass in person over five hours ago, at
church, but you didn't show up. The urgent information
ain't have nothing to do with grandma, her account is
closed, insurance claim paid." Sheila paused like she was
being hesitant.

Mattie rinsed her mouth off and put the toothbrush in the
holder before taking her rag to get the remaining toothpaste
of her mouth.

"Well Lala, are you going to tell me? Just spit it out."

Mattie looked for her cosmetic bag to put something onto her face to cover the bruising.

"I'm gonna be an auntie." Sheila said without any emotion.

"You're going to be an auntie, what? Which one of your brothers have got some chick knocked up now, no matter how much we tell em they just don't listen, use some damn protection?" Mattie paused as she searched for the tour schedule.

"No woman, your ass is embarazada, pregnant, with child." Sheila said excitedly a second time.

Mattie stared into the mirror holding the tour dates in her hand.

"Pregnant, who pregnant?" Mattie asked, she hadn't really been paying attention.

"You are, the blood tests don't lie, now I get to tell them broads because they been asking me all day what I knew, but I ain't gon tell nobody else. Are you ok? Mattie say something." Sheila asked concerned that the revelation was too much.

Mattie felt numb, she recalled the tests they ran when she passed out the day her grandmother died, but thought nothing of them.

"Mattie, what are you thinking about?" Sheila asked again with concern.

Mattie wasn't sure exactly what she was thinking.

Her birth control wasn't effective and she wasn't prepared to bring a child into the world were her first thoughts.

She sat down, and visions of motherhood flashed before her; a child with Kendal. She loved him and it would make him happy to bring a child into this world that was his own flesh and blood.

Sheila remained silent, understanding that her friend had suffered emotional stress on levels most couldn't fathom. Her friend's life would change, she would come face to face with the comparisons she would make to her own mother.

Mattie felt light-headed even as she sat, hearing the news

created uncertainty inside her. She knew there were two definite actions to take, so as Sheila cleared her throat, Mattie answered her friend's question.

"Dr. Stevens and I are going to have to sort some shit out, because honestly I feel numb, so that's my first call, and the second thing on my list is to buy an airline ticket to New York. I want to see Kendal's face when he hears he is going to be a daddy." She rubbed her belly this time knowing the reason why she felt nauseous.

Sheila reinforced that she would be a great mother before telling Mattie she was calling Geri and Cindy. Mattie knew her friends would keep her secret until she was ready to share it with others.

After ending the call, Mattie walked into the bathroom and stared into the mirror. She touched the bruises on her face and her ribs where she had been kicked. She wondered if her life experience prepared her for being called 'mom'.

Aunt Penny would be told, but only after her appointment with Dr. Stevens.

Mattie placed both of her hands across her belly and realized that life had been created inside her. After the circumstances of facing death, she thought it ironic that the Universe had filled her with life.

"The Universe does not make mistakes."

ABOUT THE AUTHOR

A.V. Smith is an athlete turned writer. During the mid-2000's, he was a featured poet at the Columbus Arts Festival and also won second place during The Great Debaters poetry slam in Columbus, Ohio as Oprah Winfrey's movie was being released nationally. With a passion for storytelling, he paints with words that draw readers into the story. A.V. writes on an emotional level to empower readers to engage in deeper conversations about their past, their relationships, and their connection with The Universe. With his first book, *Madison God's Fingerprint 1.618,* he won the Author Academy award for Best Romance in 2019. He recently released two crime novels, *OHIO 10* and *OHIO 10 Book II.* A.V. will also release a fantasy fiction book soon under pseudonym J. B. White in recognition of his elders.

Through life and love, A.V. has learned our journeys are temporary, yet intensely meaningful. This understanding led him to donate a kidney to his younger brother. As the father of three children, his desire is to see his children overcome the fear of success by being the best version of themselves; therefore, he strives to lead by example, at times falling short, but understanding human beings are still a work in progress. When he is not engaged in his passion, you can find him with a fishing pole in his hand, coaching youth level football, or attending a local artist event.

For more information, please visit
www.warpedwritingandpublishing.com.

Other Books by A.V. Smith

Madison: God's Fingerprint 1.618

While in College, Madison befriends a second-generation Colombian who gets bullied until she steps in. Madison receives more than a simple warm welcome when her friend takes her to visit Colombia for his family's gratitude. Unbeknownst to Madison, a familial bond is illuminated that changes her future. Love dares to awaken Madison's soul; however, with the darkness that surrounded her teenage years, she has constructed walls of protection.

As passionate, erotic themes and emotional conflict shift her vision of the world, she is forced to face the event that paralyzed her father and sent her parents to prison. The murder of a family of three combined with a harassing phone call at work puts Madison on a collision course with the man who had her friend's father assassinated, and who tainted the narcotics found in her father's possession the night her life was forever changed. Madison is a woman with a tumultuous past struggling to escape her demons all the while blindsided by love at a poetry event. Longing to feel normal, Madison attempts to balance her desire for justice with her need for swift, deadly punishment. With the help of her grandmother and sister-friends, she discovers who she really is as well as the courage to let love in.

Madison: In the Presence of God

Madison continues on her journey of vulnerability and intimacy. She learns to submit to her fears as things between her and Kendal take a turn. Madison explores the depths of her sexuality with a man who pushes her physical limits, but intimacy requires trust. Is she ready? Is she willing?

In the meantime, tragedy strikes, and Madison is forced to defend her family. In so doing, she is steps closer to revealing who her true enemy is and why.

OHIO 10

A story about good cops versus bad cops amidst a crooked, criminal, and political regime. Based in the capital city of Ohio, the stories surround a diverse group of Columbus detectives. Against all odds the team takes on the inestimable task of maintaining integrity and staying alive while bringing the city to justice from top to bottom.

OHIO 10 Book II

In part one of OHIO 10, Author A.V. Smith acquainted readers with a team of Columbus detectives and the cases they closed. In OHIO 10 Book II, everything escalates with even bigger stakes at hand.

Personal challenges mount for each member of the team as they investigate City Hall, and the crooked law enforcement officials that oversee the city. Two detectives are tasked to go deep in an undercover assignment. Will they be discovered?

Pressures increase for Captain Montgomery to stop investigating cold cases. As the team wars against crime, they learn their toughest battles aren't on the streets, but in the rank and file. The same people who swore to uphold the law are in the pocket of a criminal mastermind. Will they each survive or find out that the force they battle is too great?

www.ingramcontent.com/pod-product-compliance
Lightning Source LLC
Chambersburg PA
CBHW070211260626
47160CB00002B/521